This story has been written by Seth Fenter, an 11 year old school boy who lives in Scarborough, North East England.

CONTENTS

Chapter 1- The Argument pg 4

Chapter 2- The Houses pg 18

Chapter 3- Painting birds pg 35

Chapter 4- Lions versus Snakes pg 44

Chapter 5- Mr and Mrs Olfankos pg 56

Chapter 6- The Elf Chamber pg 74

Chapter 7- The Elf Dinner pg 98

Chapter 8- Mr Slake's Detention pg 109

Chapter 9- The Spelling Bee pg 118

Chapter 10- The Unexpected Arrival pg 133

Chapter 11- The Dragon Cave pg 150

Chapter 12- Sacked pg 161

Chapter 13- Christmas Day pg 175

Chapter 14- Doluffid Potion pg 184

Chapter 15- Slake's Revenge pg 195

Chapter 16- The Tonkfar & the Hospital pg 207

Chapter 17- Frangini's Warning pg 217

Chapter 1- The Argument

It was a sunny Thursday afternoon but the breeze was cold. All was silent and peaceful, right up to the minute that the bell of St Rickmoor primary school rang loudly for the end of the day, and loads of kids aged between 5 to 11 years came rushing out of the building. But after all that mayhem it was soon peaceful again. In the large school of Rickmoor, the classrooms were empty except for a very few children and teachers. One of the children was a dark-haired boy with bright blue eyes, his name was Frank Burray, who actually wanted to be at school and was dreading the summer holidays.

His mother had been brutally murdered when he was a baby and shortly after, his father had gone missing, presumed dead. Ever since those tragic events he had to live with his Grampa Joe and Grandma Molly. They both hated him just as much as Frank hated them. Even though they had a big 3 bedroom house they didn't let Frank have his own bedroom. They made him sleep in the shed - a cold, restless place, which sadly he'd had to make into a home for himself. He spent all his time in the shed and he didn't really have any friends.

At half-past four, he was told to go home. As usual, he went the long way home along the beach, through the forest and past the park. He always walked really slowly, normally picking a stone from the front of the school to kick it all the way home. He got to his house at quarter-past five to find his Grampa and Grandma waiting for him.

"*We* are going out for tea tonight. *You* will be staying in that shed. Just because you're such a brat we're going to lock the shed door," said Grampa Joe smugly. (Frank hated watching Grampa Joe talk because when his wrinkly lips opened Frank could see his dirty brownish teeth.)

At seven o'clock, Grampa Joe and Grandma Molly, clutching their walking sticks tightly, came down the old wooden staircase. Grandma Molly was wearing a red dress which had old food stains down the front of it, and too much make-up was smudged all over her pasty, wrinkled face. Frank could smell her cloying, sickly sweet perfume when she she was about a dozen paces away from him. Grampa Joe was wearing an old, tatty, dark coloured suit with frayed cuffs which made him look fat. He also had a greasy blue tie, with mouldy, green spots on it and was too tight around his neck making his face all red.

"Now young man, if I were you then I'd stay in t'shed," Grampa Joe muttered while checking in the hall mirror if his tie was straight.

Frank went into the small shed and heard the front door slam and lock. He then realised that they hadn't locked the shed or the back door - he could get into the house! He waited for a few minutes to hear their car's tyres crunch over the weed infested gravel of the driveway as they left. He didn't hesitate, he ran out of the shed and went into the house through the back door. He turned the TV on and got some crisps and toffees. At twenty-past seven he saw lights outside, it was Grampa Joe's car parking up. Frank now had so many thoughts in his head. Why are they back so early? Have they had an argument and come home? Frank put Comedy Old Show on, the show that Grampa Joe likes to watch, turned the TV off and locked the back door. He heard the door open. He realised that he was so stupid, he had locked himself in the house not in the shed. He hid behind the table and watched not four but eight feet go into the kitchen. Frank then heard Grampa Joe open the back door. He was going to check on the shed. Without thinking, Frank picked up the closest thing he could see and launched it into the front room. It was a large boot, black and dusty but it crashed and made a thundering sound. Everyone ran into the front room, including Grampa Joe which left Frank enough time to get outside into the shed.

"What have you done?" shouted Grampa Joe while storming into the dark shed.

"I- I didn't do anything! I've been here since you left," said Frank trying to look innocent.

Grampa Joe's mouth went crinkly and said, "Look, turns out their house is being decorated so we have to have our tea here. Now you do not leave this shed until tomorrow morning. Do you understand?" before Frank could answer, Grampa Joe had slammed the mouldy shed door and stamped up to the house's back door, which he also slammed out of annoyance.

Frank tried to find something to entertain himself, Grandma Molly always had a cake in the fridge and she always took absolutely ages to eat it. Frank then thought – how about he went to just have a peek at what kind of cake it was?

He silently opened the shed door, quietly crept upto the house and peeked through the dining room window. On the table in there was an apple pie with hot steaming custard with plates and spoons all set out neatly. He then went to look through the kitchen window and saw the remains of their meal on all the plates. They had had steak, one of Frank's favourite meals. Frank then went to look in the front room, he saw Grampa Joe, a man with a moustache wearing a black suit and a red tie,and an old looking woman, around 60 who had glasses on. Grampa Joe turned his head towards Frank but luckily didn't spot him. Grandma Molly then got up out of her seat and started walking towards the kitchen. She then pulled out a a large strawberry flavoured cake out of the cupboard. The cake looked amazing. It had four layers of strawberry sponge cake on top of each other and green, orange and yellow icing on each of the layers. She then lifted her weak arms onto the bottom of the plate and put it on the table in the dining room. She went back into the front room and watched the last drop of champagne drip into her glass. Frank couldn't resist it, they wouldn't realise if he just had a teeny bit of the cake, would they?

He opened the back door, he could hear Grandma Molly's high pitched fake laugh in the front room and low voices talking. He crawled into the dining room and saw the glamorous cake next to the warm apple pie and custard. He only got a bit of cake, then he got another little bit, then another...then Frank took a big lump of cake and the whole thing came apart. Half of it went into the apple pie and the other half went *splat* on the floor. It didn't make too much of a noise, but made a sound that the next room couldn't hear.

Frank then heard Grampa Joe say, "Molly has been in the kitchen all day making an outstanding cake that she was going to bring to your house with us - but the silly woman forgot to! But not to worry - we can have a thick slice each now! I made an apple pie as well with this really creamy custard. Come on then, lets go and have our pudding."

Frank didn't hesitate, he ran as fast as he could but trying not to make any noise at all. He got straight into bed and heard Grampa Joe's booming voice shouting something but couldn't hear what. He heard a car starting and presumed it was…he couldn't think, then he heard the back door open and close. Frank turned his back to the door as it was flung open by Grampa Joe, and the shed light flickered on. Frank heard him whisper to someone, probably Grandma Molly, then the light was turned off and the door shut, only this time he locked it.

It took Frank so long to get to sleep. He had so many questions in his head, what would Grampa Joe do in the morning? Would he even let him go to school? Would he lock the door again? Frank turned over and saw it was nearly three in the morning. Eventually, at around half-past three Frank fell asleep and the shed fell silent...

****

BEEP, BEEP, BEEP, it was his alarm clock. He looked what time it was, quarter to seven, he pressed snooze and just when his eyes were about to shut again - *BEEP, BEEP, BEEP* - the sound was awful so he decided to get up. He stumbled about looking for the light as it was still dark outside, and tripped over his shoe. He found the light and thought that he'd face Grampa Joe and Grandma Molly after school. He pulled out a chocolate bar and ate it for his breakfast, then he got dressed. Even though he had to get to school by quarter to nine, he set off at half-past seven and walked the long way. It was quiet in the park as there were only a few people walking their dogs and in the forest, there was wet dew on the green grass and very few birds were flying about.

On the beach, the waves were rushing over it and were

crashing up against the footpath which made it really slippery, cold and wet. It took Frank longer to get across the beach as he kept nearly slipping over. He eventually got off the beach pathway and only had to walk down another path and he was at school.

He walked even slower than he had when walking down the beach path as not even the teachers had got to school yet. When he was about half way down the footpath, cars started to zoom past Frank and park up next to Rickmoor. He then started to walk at normal pace and got to school with no one else visible for miles around. Frank looked at his watch, it was twenty-five past eight. The caretaker saw Frank waiting at the gates and surprisingly let him in earlier than usual. Frank walked into the deserted cloakroom, hung up his bag and coat and went to the toilet as he couldn't use the one at his Grandparents' house. He took the thick Harry Potter book that he was reading out of his bag and walked through the vacant corridors and into his classroom, class twenty-one. The room was empty and even his teacher hadn't got to school yet. You could hear a pin drop in the classroom. His teacher, Miss Raset, came into the class a few minutes later with a cup of coffee and an apple in her hand.

"Oh, hello Frank, you're here early today aren't you?" she said joyfully.

Frank looked out the window and saw more kids who were walking through the gates now. Frank was in Year six, the last year, and it was his last day – well, it was actually everyone's last day in Year six at Rickmoor. He was moving on to Severors Secondary School, and he was one of the only ones that were going to Severors.

****

At three minutes to three, everyone's eyes were on the clock. Three minutes...now two...until the summer holidays. Frank could hear people counting down the seconds under their breath. Even he was looking forward to the holidays - right until he remembered what had happened last night and he still hadn't faced Grampa Joe yet. He looked at his watch, there were exactly twenty-six seconds until the bell rang!

"I hope you all have a nice time at secondary school and at home in the sum-" Miss Raset's short speech was cut even shorter by the bell.

"OK bye then everyone!" Miss Raset said while letting the children out table by table, "Oh and one last thing, on your way out collect a bag, it's a present."

Frank didn't even have to look at the bag as knew what it was. A book and a chocolate egg, and he was right. Frank looked at the book, it was a book about Goblins with a picture on the front cover of an ugly looking Goblin's face which looked like a zombie.

Frank lived in Scarborough, where his mother had been born. His father had been born in Middlesbrough. Frank also liked zombies, space and anything to do with paranormal activity, and magic tricks. He wanted to be a magician when he was older, he had asked for a magic set for his birthday, on April first, (April fools day). Grampa Joe, in Frank's mind, was a total idiot. Of course, he didn't get him a magic set, he got Frank a tiny Christmas bauble and nothing else. Because there was five months till Christmas, he wasn't very happy with his present and chucked it in to a cardboard box with his other ten cheap baubles. Grampa Joe and Grandma Molly always got Frank a gaudy cheap bauble for his birthday present...

Frank got to Candlestick street and looked down the empty

street. He lived at number twenty-five. Frank walked slowly and quietly onto the driveway. He looked to his right, he saw Grampa Joe's car, and on his left he saw the next door neighbours house, Roger's. He crawled in through the back gate and tiptoed into the shed. Unfortunately, Grampa Joe heard Frank shut the shed door and came storming out of his house and into the shed.

"I know what you did last night! Now tonight you will bake a cake and you will not bother us, OK?" whispered Grampa Joe menacingly.

"Er, Why?" asked Frank.

Grampa Joe replied by saying, "Me and your Grandmother are going out for dinner with Roger tonight. Now you go make that cake."

Just as Grampa Joe turned his back Frank muttered, "No."

Grampa Joe slowly turned around, his eyes narrowed.

"What did you say to me boy?" Grampa Joe was starting to walk towards him.

Frank said savagely, "Why Should I?"

That was probably the worst mistake he had made all year.

Grampa Joe locked the shed door and locked the back door until Saturday evening, Grampa Joe fed him a bowl of mushy bananas and apples for his dinner and the same for his breakfast on Saturday morning. Frank had gone to sleep really early (eight o'clock) on Friday night and woke up around six o'clock the following morning. He thought to himself, that he had to sit there for eleven more hours.

He lay on his bed, it was still dark outside but Frank could hear cars on the next street but his was silent. Nobody was awake on Candlestick street except Frank. He looked up at Roger's windows, they were all dark. Normally, Roger would be up by now, Frank thought it was a bit weird but then he thought it was the first day of the holidays. Frank looked in another window and could see through a gap in the bush Erny's front room and his TV. Frank also liked football but he hated running, rugby and basketball. His favourite football team was Manchester United and his favourite player was Romelu Lukaku, a Belgium player.

Frank liked to play as a striker and he had played for the school team. On the Saturday morning it was Manchester United versus Chelsea and maybe if Erny put it on his TV,

Frank could watch it through the window. He waited all morning until it was on. Frank looked through the gap and saw that Erny had put the Manchester United game on. Frank ate a box of chocolates while watching. He thought he kept hearing Grampa Joe opening and closing the back door. At half-time, Grampa Joe did come outside to find him eating a box of chocolates, on his bed watching a football match.

At the end of the match, on the screen, it said:

Manchester United 3-0 Chelsea

Lukaku 35'

Lukaku 78'

Lukaku 83'

Lukaku had scored a hat trick (three goals) and had won the title of 'man of the match'. After the match Frank did not know what to do. He was so bored. He took a glance at his watch, it was three pm. Grampa Joe finally unlocked the door at five o'clock and Frank didn't question him about anything. Grampa Joe said that Roger had moved house and that he should never speak of it again. That made Frank a bit suspicious as he had not seen Roger since Grampa Joe and Grandma Molly went round to his house for dinner.

On the Monday of the second week police cars were next door, first at Erny's then he heard a policeman knock on the door of twenty-five Candlestick Street. He heard Grandma Molly open the door and shut it. He couldn't hear anything for about half an hour then he heard the police car's engine start. Frank opened the shed door and took a look through the gap in the wooden fence. He must have been imagining it, but he thought he saw Grampa Joe driving the police car, not the policeman he had seen in Erny's house. Then he had a crazy thought, he thought it was ridiculous, he can't have. Frank thought it was impossible, Grampa Joe hadn't harmed Roger or the policeman, had he?

Chapter 2- The Houses

Frank didn't have any more family except his Godfather, Shaun. He couldn't live with his Godfather as he was in the army, probably in Iraq. Frank had met him briefly when he was only four years old, when Grampa Joe had made him leave early because he'd asked why Frank lived in the shed?! He thought he would not meet his Godfather ever again - until last week when something unexpected happened.

On the last Monday of the holidays Grampa Joe came into the shed, in his hand he had a postal package that had an envelope sellotaped onto its front.

"Y've gotta parcel, and what looks like a letter. I dunno what it's about or who it's from, but it's probably from Severors," he grunted while tossing it to Frank. He then walked out of the shed, Frank heard the back door shut and he took a look at the envelope.

It said on the front:

Frank Burray
25 Candlestick Street
Scarborough, England

Frank opened the envelope first, there was a sheet of paper with blue writing on it saying,

Dear Frank,

You might remember meeting me but I wouldn't be surprised if you don't. Your Mother and Father both went to Severors Secondary School. Your Father had this book. It's in the package. The real reason I'm writing this letter is because I want to warn you about the year ahead. There are dark things hidden in Severors. If someone tells you to do something, do it, it might just save your life. The teachers' know all about the dark things hidden in the school. Now keep this book and do not lose it. The future of Severors will depend on this book. If you need to tell anyone anything important, tell the Headmaster straightaway.

I will meet you in later years,

Shaun.

Apart from being his Godfather, and being in the army - who was Shaun he thought? Frank read it all through again and then took the letter away from his face and opened the package. It was a book about Goblins. He thought he had seen the goblin on the front of the book before but he couldn't remember where. Frank looked around the shed, then he saw it. It was the same book as he had got from school on his last day there but only a bit dirtier! Frank put them both under his bed and looked out of the shed window at what Erny was watching on TV.

****

It was the night before Frank went to secondary school. He couldn't get to sleep. At around half-past one, a cold breeze flew into the shed. Frank finally decided to shut the window, and got out of his warm bed to do it. After a while the shed was still cold, but it was a little bit warmer than before. It didn't take long then for Frank to close his eyes, and doze off to sleep.

Frank woke up to his alarm beeping at quarter to seven. It was dark and cold outside. He got out of bed and waited for a few minutes and then ate an apple and a banana. Erny was up all ready but he heard nothing else. Frank checked his watch, it was twenty-eight minutes to eight. He decided to set off at twenty to eight, he had to walk a different way as he wasn't walking to Rickmoor. He walked through the woods, past the beach, past the park, past the football pitch and he was there. There were actually quite a few kids there already. The gates opened at eight o'clock and everyone walked in. Frank looked around the cloakroom. He saw a peg marked, **_FRANK BURRAY._**

He walked into his registration class and saw on the big whiteboard, **_House Ceremony - 8.30_** and it was underlined several times.

He then looked to the right and saw a man, he had dark hair with glasses on and had a black moustache. He was wearing a black suit and a white shirt with an orange tie around his thin neck.

There were post-it notes in every seat with names on. Frank looked at a few before he got to his seat, **_ERIC MONSHAUL, DAVID GAUKHAN, HARRY THOMTS._** Those were just a few names, he found his seat right at the back of the classroom. At a quarter-past past eight, nearly every seat was occupied. Frank was looking around the classroom when he heard someone next to him ask, "What's 'the house ceremony'?"

Frank looked in the direction of the boy who had just spoken to him. He had blonde hair and a confused look on his face.

Frank replied by saying, "I don't know. What's your name?"

Frank looked down to his post-it note. He could just make out his name even though the boy had doodled on it, it was *'Peter Puginic'*.

Just then he heard another voice but it was a girl's voice this time. "It's where you're split into one of the three houses."

Frank looked over and saw her. She had brown, bushy hair with hazel eyes.

"But what are houses? I mean – 'course I know what a house is but, *what do they mean here?!"* asked Peter.

The girl replied by saying, "You'll just have to wait and see."

Frank saw that she was called **'Lucy Dart'** but just when he was about to ask her what school she was from, the man he'd seen earlier - he must be the teacher, stood up.

He cleared his throat noisily and said, "Hello class! My name is Mr Anderson and I will be taking you down to the house ceremony after doing the register - now no talking while I do the register."

He sat back down and looked at his computer screen for the list of names. After the register it was twenty-five minutes past eight, Mr Anderson got back up out of his seat again. He cleared his throat noisily again and said, "Now everyone line up at the door and come with me."

He then opened the door and led everyone out. The corridors were large and tall. He walked them down to the middle of the school and into a hall. The hall was massive and the walls were painted in bright orange, light green and dark brown. Frank then looked back at the doors he had just walked through, it was amazing. The back wall was split into 3 sections of the same colours that were on the other walls, orange, green and brown. Frank was so distracted by the walls and colours that he didn't spot the tables that were neatly set out. The tables had four seats each set out next to them. Even the floor was decorated in orange, green and brown. Mr Anderson sat them all down on a bench seat next to the stage and they waited until everyone else came in.

Finally, the room was packed with children and teachers. All the teachers were sat on the stage and there was an old, ornate wooden chair right in the middle. Everyone was whispering until the man who was sitting in that chair, who had a short, brown beard and well brushed short brown hair stood up and

and shouted, "Silence!"

His voice sounded like it could have been heard from miles away! "My name is Mr Cuewant and I am your headmaster. As all you older kids know, it's time for the house ceremony - and I can't wait for it. Now, for the benefit of the children who have just arrived today, I will explain. The house ceremony is a tradition that Severors has done for many years. There are 3 houses, the Lions are orange, the Snakes are green and the brown are Scorpions. When I call your name out, you will stand in one of the three squares on the stage. You will look above you, and a trapdoor will open and either an orange, green or brown shirt will fall upon you. If you get brown you will go sit with the children will the brown shirts on, green you sit with green and orange you sit with orange. Oh and the shirts will turn above the stage so you will not be able to see which colour shirts are above whichever trapdoor you pick and when the shirts come down you will pick one up and put it on, you will be split evenly."

That got everyone excited, Mr Cuewant was then handed a sheet of paper and he said, *"Amanda Boghont."*

She got up out of her seat.

"Now pick a trapdoor," Mr Cuewant said while smiling at her.

She went to the right hand side and a drum started to bang. All the older children started to bang on the table so the younger kids started to bang on their knees. The drum stopped, the older kids stopped and the younger kids stopped. The trapdoor opened and brown shirts came tumbling onto her, all the Scorpions cheered and clapped. She picked up a brown shirt and sat down. Mr Cuewant said a few other names then Frank heard a familiar name, *"Peter Puginic."*

Peter was sat next to Frank and he saw that his face went red. He got up out of his seat and walked towards the stage where Mr Cuewant was standing. "Now Peter, you've seen other people do it. Just wait a second, the shirts need to rotate above the stage."

Before Frank could even raise his eyebrows, there was a loud horrible sound. It was like a rattling old car engine but with your ear pressed right next to it. The sound suddenly stopped and Mr Cuewant whispered to Peter, "Go on, go pick a square."

Peter went straight to the middle. The drums began to bang and the children began to bang. They stopped again and orange shirts drenched Peter. *"LIONS!"* shouted Mr Cuewant.

The Lions clapped and cheered and Peter went to sit down. Mr Cuewant cleared his throat again and said loud and clearly, *"Sam Matthews."*

A boy from the front row stood up, he had white hair and a pale, white face. Frank saw that the sunlight was streaming through the windows and shining upon him, and he was whimpering. He stood up and went to the stage, the rattling sound started up again. He went to the left and the drum started again. It stopped and green shirts brought him to the ground. *"Snakes!"* roared Mr Cuewant.

The Snakes all loudly hissed this time and then they all clapped. A few more names were called out and then Frank heard a name that he recognised, *"Lucy Dart."*

She got up out of her seat and walked towards Mr Cuewant. She picked the middle square. The orange shirts fell onto her. *"LIONS!"* Mr Cuewant bellowed.

After five minutes of watching people getting drenched in shirts, Frank was getting anxious. There were only ten people left waiting to find out what house they were in. Before Frank could even look up he heard, *"Frank Burray."* Frank was petrified.

It didn't look so hard watching but when he went up he thought to himself, *whichever one I picked I'll be in that house for six years'.* He decided to pick the one on the right. Frank was sweating until the orange shirts fell upon him. He was so relieved, he then heard, *"LIONS!"* but Mr Cuewant was cut short from the roars from the lions.

Frank sat down next to Peter, Harry (Harry had been at Rickmoor school with Frank and was now in Lions as well) and Lucy. Mr Anderson put a microphone on the stage and everyone waited. Mr Cuewant stood up and his voice echoed across the room.

"Before we all go back to class, I would like to make an announcement...I would like to give a warm Severor's welcome to our two new teachers who are starting today. Mrs Walliams will be our new caretaker of the school and I am happy to present Mr Slake as our new deputy head teacher, Head of Snakes, and a Maths' teacher. Oh and one last thing, you will all be given a timetable today. Now everyone get to the class you're suppose to be in, *no* dawdling and no talking!"

First the Scorpions left, then Snakes and then Lions. Just before Frank was about to leave, Mr Cuewant pulled him out the crowd. "Frank, meet me in my office at half-past nine."

Frank saw on his watch that it was twenty-three minutes past nine and when he looked back up, Mr. Cuewant had gone. At first he thought he was in trouble, but it was a lot different than that. He saw the sign on his door it said, ***M. CUEWANT HEADMASTER OFFICE.*** Frank knocked, no reply, so he went in and sat down, opposite to the wooden chair tucked in behind the large desk. He looked at his watch, it was thirty-three minutes past nine. Just then, Mr Cuewant walked in and said, "Sorry I'm a bit late. Now, that book, the Goblin one, do not lose it, OK? I shan't tell you why until you're a bit older, you might not understand right now, just do not lose it, *Do You Understand*?"

"Yes Sir," Frank said.

"Now you may leave, off you go." Mr Cuewant said with a grin on his face (a happy grin).

Frank stood up and walked towards the door, opened it, stepped out and shut it. Then something came into his mind: Shaun had told him to not lose the book and *If someone tells you to do something, do it, it might just save your life'.* That made Frank decide that he would definitely not lose it, whatever happened he would not let it out of his sight. He could hear distant shouting but the corridor he was walking down was silent. Mr Anderson had said to meet in his classroom so Frank walked towards his class. It was nearly ten o'clock when he got there. Frank opened the door, Mr Anderson was handing out timetable sheets.

"Come on Frank, sit down, sit." he said.

Frank walked over to his seat, he could hear the howling wind outside and the heavy rain which was pounding on the old windows of Severors Secondary School. Mr Anderson gave Frank his timetable. The first thing Frank saw on the spreadsheet printout was: ***10AM MATHS/ TEACHER: MR SLAKE.***

"Now everyone, hurry up and get to your class before everyone else is allowed out!" Mr Anderson chuckled.

Everyone hurried out of the classroom but it was too late. The corridors had been overtaken by kids with either green, orange or brown shirts on. Just then, Frank realised that he had left his shirt in the Enchanted Hall. (That's what all the teachers called it.) He decided to run as fast as he could back to the hall. Half way down the long corridor, Frank noticed he would be late for Maths. His favourite class was Maths, he got to the hall at two minutes to ten. He saw his shirt and clutched it in his hand, but just when he was about to leave, he bumped into a large man.

"An' where d'ya think yar goin'?" the large man barked.

Frank looked up at him, he looked like a giant. "Umm, I-I'm heading off to my maths class," he answered.

"Now look at this board," the man growled.

He was pointing towards a golden board saying: *SEVEROR'S RULES YOU SHALL NOT BREAK!* Frank saw the first one was: *NO RUNNING INSIDE THE SCHOOL!*

"Do y'a undastand that eh?" the giant said.

Frank was so petrified that he didn't even notice that he said, "Yes, Sir! Sorry!"

The man then walked off, saying he was on his way to Mr Cuewant's office. He had one minute to get to Maths. Frank didn't care if the giant gave him detention, he just didn't want to be… but he was - late. His watch was beeping so that meant it was ten o'clock. Frank ran past Mr Anderson's class but saw something in his place. He quickly ran in and had a look what it was, **FRANK BURRAY TIMETABLE**, it said on the the top of the sheet. Frank grabbed it and ran, while he was running he put on his orange shirt. Frank had not yet realised it had a picture of a fierce lion on the front. He got to Mr Slake's classroom and when he opened the door he saw him waiting for him.

"Always one, isn't there?! You're fifty two seconds late, that's a detention," Mr Slake had an evil, wicked grin on his face.

Mr Slake had a small moustache and black hair. He wore a black cloak and black trousers with black shoes.

"Dear boy sit, you shall sit at the front where I can see you," he said in a frightening voice.

Frank was in the worst place possible, he had been shouted (well not shouted at, stopped) by the giant, and now he'd been shouted at by Mr Slake.

"Now, what is 95,273 x 42? work it out, NOW!" Slake bellowed at the class.

A boy in green shot his hand up.

"What is it?" asked Slake in a grumpy voice.

"Is it 4,001,466, sir?" he asked.

"Pass me a calculator, now what might your name be?" Slake asked.

"My name is Johnny Devas, sir," the boy answered.

It looked like Mr Slake was getting impatient, "SOMEBODY PASS ME A CALCULATOR!" he shouted.

Peter's hand shot up.

"What?" spat Slake.

"Where are the calculators, sir?" he added, Mr Slake pointed towards a box next to the door.

"QUICKLY!" Slake shouted.

Nobody dared to move, "What is your name?" he whispered to Frank.

"Frank, Frank Burray," he was petrified.

"Well Burray, GET ME A CALCULATOR!" Mr Slake was getting really impatient.

Frank got up out of his seat and walked over to the calculators. He got one out and passed it to Mr Slake. Their hands slightly touched, Slake's hand was cold and it paralysed Frank's whole body for a second or two.

"Sit," Mr Slake said narrowing his eyes.

Frank heard Mr Slake muttering "95,273 x 42" under his dark voice.

"Correct, Mr Devas. YOU'RE ALL TO SLOW!" Mr Slake shouted.

He wrote some more sums on the board.

"Work them all out before the break," he said and sat down, there were 10 sums.

43587 x 56

3458 x 20

5769 x 47

And seven more like that, Frank answered the first one but couldn't help wondering what Mr Slake was doing. Just then, Mr Slake put his head up and looked straight at Frank.

"Get on with your sums, Burray." he said.

When Mr Slake put his head down Frank put his head back up, it looked like he was writing a note to someone. Frank saw that he had twenty minutes left to do the multiplication sums. He got up to the seventh question when a fire alarm started, at first Frank thought that it was his watch but it was much louder. "Everyone line up, *SENSIBLY*," Mr Slake said loudly over to the tumultuous sound.

A man then ran in and shouted, "FIRE! FIRE!"

Mr Slake responded by saying, "Oh shut up you fool! It's probably just a fake."

That send everybody crazy. Nearly everyone started screaming but Mr Slake soon put a stop to that, "SILENT! IT WILL BE A PRACTICE! Rilge, get out and everyone walk outside immediately."

Chapter 3- Painting Birds

After Mr Cuewant came out of the school building and told everyone it was a fake, it was well into the break time. Just when Frank started walking towards Peter, he heard a cold voice saying, "Burray, where do you think your going? Have you forgotten about detention, because I haven't," it was Slake. "Come with me, I've got a little job for you, it's not too big.

"Collect all the books in, except yours, you will finish yours before I get back or I will give you a week of detentions." Mr Slake said loudly to him as they entered the classroom.

He then left the classroom and all was nearly silent in the room, but he could hear some distant screams coming from the playground, and he could hear the clock on the wall ticking loudly while he collected the books in. Mr Cuewant then walked in and asked, "Oh, is Mr Slake in here? Why are you in here Frank?" he asked curiously.

"I was fifty-two seconds late to class," Frank said.

"I heard that you didn't realise not to run and you were in a rush. When Shadrik, our giant who you bumped into, stopped you, that took a lot of your time off, so go on, out to break, I'll put the books away." Mr Cuewant said smiling.

"*Wow!* Thank you," Frank said with a perplexed look on his face.

When Frank was walking out to the playground he looked at his timetable to see what was next after the break.

11AM ART/ TEACHER: MRS ROSE.

When Frank was walking through the doors to the playground, he didn't notice that someone was going to crash into him...***CRASH!*** Frank went flying into a pile of coats while the other boy stayed standing. Frank looked up, a boy with a green shirt on stood above him.

"Watch where your going, loser," he said pulling a face and laughing with his two friends behind him.

"Why don't you?" Frank said getting up.

Frank couldn't stop himself, before he could even think what to do next, his foot was already behind his back and in mid air. He then kicked it forward with all his might and swung it round the back of the boy's leg. The boy tumbled into his friend in front of him and cried out in pain, "I'M DYING! SOMEONE HELP ME, I'M DYING!"

Unfortunately, Mr Slake was walking past right at the very moment Frank kicked the boy. Mr Slake saw Frank and shouted, *"Why are you out of detention?"*

At that moment, Frank looked towards the boy and saw his two friends that were still standing had started to walk towards him. He didn't hesitate, he ran out of the doors into the playground. The playground was huge! There were so many hiding places but just as he was looking for a good one he bumped into someone: Peter.

"Oh, hi Frank, where've you been? I've been looking for you all over," Peter said.

"Tell you later," Frank shouted while running away.

His voice echoed across the playground, and only when Frank had got to the place most far away from the cloakrooms as possible, did he breathe a sigh of relief. Only for about three seconds though as the bell rang. He joined a big crowd of boys going through the cloakroom so they couldn't see him.

Unluckily, Mr Slake was waiting for him outside the cloakroom, along with the boy he'd kicked. He grabbed Frank by the arm and dragged him along the corridor, he got to Mr

Cuewant's office and knocked on the door.

Mr Cuewant opened it and said: "Luke, I let Frank out of detention, oh good morning Jack Shaw, good morning Frank, again. Luke, you get back to Maths and I'll sort these boys out."

Frank was so relived that Mr Cuewant wanted to talk to him, not Slake.

"What happened here?" asked Mr Cuewant, still with a big smile on his face.

"Jack, you tell your side of the story first," Mr Cuewant said to Jack- the boy who Frank kicked.

Jack's side of the story was very different from reality.

"Thank you Jack, you may leave," Mr Cuewant said quietly.

Jack left with a massive smug smile on his face. "You may leave as well Frank," he then said.

Frank was really confused, "Oh, before you do - can I see your arm first Frank?" Mr Cuewant asked while brushing his hair out of his eyes.

Frank had not looked at his arm from when he went flying

into the pile of coats and bags. Frank saw on Mr Cuewant's desk there was a bottle of water with a label wrapped around it reading: *LIQUID MEMORY WATER.*

"Before I show you my arm, what is that?" asked Frank nodding towards the bottle.

Mr Cuewant turned around and said, "That? It's my drinking water, it has that label on because the shop is called Liquid Memory bed shop, they sell water because they need more money. Now lets see that arm shall we?"

Frank lifted up his jumper and saw that there was a scar on his arm that had opened up, and it was bleeding a little bit, which made it look and feel even worse. Mr Cuewant patted it gently - and to Frank's amazement the bleeding stopped!

"It won't kill you, you'll live," he chuckled.

"Off you go, Frank. You'll be late to class," Mr Cuewant said getting out of chair and opening the door.

Frank muttered "Wow! Thanks for that, how...?!" but Mr Cuewant ignored his question, and just smiled quickly at him before returning to his desk. Frank walked out the door and into the corridor, he heard the door shut as he started to walk down to the art class. He could see Jack at the end of the long corridor but no one else was in the hallway. Frank thought, why had Mr Cuewant only wanted to hear Jack's story, not his? It's like he already knew what had happened, but how? There were no cameras in the cloakroom, well as far as he knew. When Frank got to the art class, Mrs Rose, a small lady with brown, curly hair with strips of ginger in it, was waiting for him, just like Mr Slake. "Get in, look what time it is!" she shrieked.

Frank looked at his watch, "It's only 10.56, we're suppose to start at eleven o'clock, miss." he said.

"What did you say to me boy? For your information, I'm a 'MRS'! Not a 'Miss' and I start as soon as everyone's in! Your art is much more precious than anything else, isn't it?" she bellowed.

"Well no, miss, Mrs I mean." Frank was getting annoyed.

"SIT! YOU UNGRATEFUL CHILD!" she spat.

When Frank was going to the last seat at the front he heard her mutter, "Little swine."

"I'M NOT A SWINE!" Frank bellowed, he felt more angry

than ever.

Frank even whispered, "Miss."

Mrs Rose slightly looked behind her shoulder and said very softly, "twelve-thirty, my office. NOW SIT!"

Frank sat down and looked around the room. Every set of eyes were on Frank. Mrs Rose turned around and screamed, "EYES ON THE BOARD!"

Everyone Frank looked at, he didn't recognise, and now everyone's eyes were on the board. Mrs Rose picked up a thick, black whiteboard pen and did some squiggles on the board. She kept swapping pens but writing the same word: *Snilbog*. Finally, she stopped writing that but then with a very squeaky pen she wrote, __**BIRDS**__ and underlined it several times.

"Everyone, draw a bird, then write down ten different kind of birds." she said while going to her desk to sit down.

Frank drew a picture of a seagull and wrote down ten kinds of birds. Mrs Rose was now quietly walking around the classroom, Frank hadn't been aware of that until she snatched his paper of him.

"A SEAGULL IS NOT A BIRD!" Mrs Rose screamed.

"What?! Yes It Is! A seagull has wings and a beak, it can fly as well - so it's a bird!" Frank argued.

"Detention for arguing with a teacher," Mrs Rose answered back.

"I've already got detention," Frank said.

"Double Detention Then!" Mrs Rose had an evil smile on her face. "A seagull is not a bird," she said while putting her fingers on the top of the page. "Say that it's not a bird, Frank, or I will rip this sheet up," Mrs Rose said crinkling her nose.

"No," Frank thought that was his worst mistake of the day, but luckily something unexpected happened.

Mr Slake and Mr Cuewant walked in, "Oh hello Mrs Rose, are we interrupting something?" Mr Cuewant said.

"No, of course not," she said placing the sheet onto her desk.

"What is that, in your hand?" asked Mr Slake very slowly.

"Oh it's just Frank's wonderful piece of art work, I was just showing it to the class and, here you go, Frank," she said narrowing her eyes while giving it back so that Mr Cuewant and Mr Slake couldn't see.

"Oh good, well, I've just come was to say that the first football match of the season will be taking place on Wednesday next week, *Lions versus Snakes.*" said Mr Cuewant happily.

"Some of you may play for the football team next year, you will just watch this year," Mr Slake told the kids.

"You may carry on with your lesson, Mrs Rose," Mr Cuewant said while walking outside of the classroom.

At half-past twelve, Frank went to Mrs Rose's office.

"Hello Frank, now I've thought about you punishment, write out, *I mustn't be late and argue with teachers,* oh...what shall I say? Er...200 times!" she said and then walked out of the room.

Chapter 4 - Lions versus Snakes

The week of the football match came fast. Even though Frank had to do his homework every night with Grampa Joe checking he was still in the shed every thirty minutes, nothing could stop Frank from being exited about the match. At Severor's school the corridors had been covered with orange and green decorations.

On Tuesday afternoon, there was a letter given out to each pupil by their class teachers saying that you could come to school on the day of the match wearing all green or all orange clothes. When Frank was back in the shed, he looked inside the large cupboard's drawers where he stuffed all his clothes. He pulled out his normal orange shirt that he wore at school and chucked it at the door for the following day, he found an old pair of green shorts and socks and did the same. He was really surprised when he found a tin of orange paint in the corner amongst a pile of other tins of decorating paints! He went to sleep at half-past seven that night but set his alarm for six o'clock.

He awoke at the beeping sound of the alarm, and ate a banana for his breakfast. Then he crept into the house for some water.

Back in the shed he opened the tin of orange paint, dipped the fingers of one hand in and then wiped them all over his face!

Frank looked in the cracked mirror on the wall – yep, one bright orange face! He ran to school, ignoring the pedestrians who stopped and stared at him in surprise, and when he got there, he went straight to the notice board. It said that the match was to start at one o'clock. Quite a few of the other Lions had also painted their faces as well, so Frank didn't feel like the odd one out.

No one really paid much attention to the morning's classes and at lunchtime, everyone was even more exited. When they only had to wait fifteen more minutes, everyone went inside early to get the register done. Mr Anderson led Frank's class outside and into the stands and seats: the football pitch looked incredible – just like a real stadium! The seats were orange and green and everyone was split into their houses. There were four stands of seats: one for snakes; one for lions; one for scorpions and one for the teachers and staff.

"Go and sit with your house and stay seated until the match starts," Mr Anderson shouted.

Everyone ran to their house seats except Frank, Peter and

Lucy, who walked.

"What do you think the score will be?" Frank asked them.

Peter bet two-one to Lions, Lucy thought it would be three-three. Frank, however, bet four-three to Lions. The game kicked off at one o'clock just as scheduled, people were cheering and booing, and like Frank, a lot of them had painted their faces with their team's colours. The atmosphere was amazing but it died down a bit at half time, a big banner fell down in front of the teachers' stand. It read:

HALF TIME

LIONS 2-2 SNAKES

CERT 11'

TRANK 36'

RUGER 40'

YULE 44'

Lions had gone two-nil up but in the last five minutes of the first half they had conceded two goals, one to Oliver Ruger (a large boy in his third year) and one to Marcus Yule (another boy in his third year).

The second half came round quickly and then everyone was back up out of their seats cheering and shouting. It was very unlucky for a boy in the stands who was knocked out when the heavy ball hit him on the head. It had been powerfully kicked by a player for the Lions but a strong breeze of wind had made it fly even faster into the stands! There were only 15 minutes left until full time when something very weird and unlucky happened. A boy in defence for the Lions tried to kick the ball out of the goal area but instead he kicked it with his left foot and put it right into the back of the Lions own goal! All the snakes roared with laughter at the error, and now it was 3 - 2 to the Snakes. All the Lions went to the floor in disbelief but then something in the last three minutes happened. The commentator was shouting through his big megaphone: *"Youth, Cert, Youth again, Trank, Ling, Ling crosses the ball into the box, Cert heads the ball, it goes over the goalkeeper and...GOAL! IT'S THREE-THREE!"*

All of the Lions were now up on their feet cheering at the top of their voices. Frank looked over to the teachers stand, Mr Slake was sitting down, looking glum as usual but all the other teachers were on their feet clapping. Frank looked back at the pitch, the match had already started again. Snakes were on the attack when Gareth the commentator shrieked: "WE'RE BEING ATTACKED! WE'RE UNDER ATTACK!"

Everyone looked into the sky, all except the football players. "Oh don't be such a fool Gareth, it's just some birds, children," Mr Slake shouted above all the noise.

Frank heard the whistle blow, it was full-time! All the other Lions thought the same but their cheers were cut short by the laughs of the Snakes. Frank looked back at the pitch, and realised it wasn't full-time – it was a penalty given to the Snakes! A dark haired boy took the ball from the referee and placed it on the now very muddy, penalty spot. He stepped three paces back, then ran a bit too fast to the ball, curved it and fell over as it thundered against the crossbar. The Lions cheered in relief when a defender kicked the ball down the pitch. The Snakes defenders were running back but couldn't catch the Lions fast running striker. His legs were bouncing across the muddy pitch, he got into the box and when he was about to shoot and score, a big Snakes defender made a crunching tackle which at first looked like it might have broken his leg. The defender got a red card and the Lions striker was stretchered off injured. Frank saw their captain, 'Dover' take the ball and place it on the penalty spot. The Lions supporters almost couldn't watch - this penalty was vital! If he scored, the Lions would win the match and go to the top of the Severor's League table. Frank was sweating, not only because of the sun beating down on him but because of how tense the match was. Dover ran to the ball and...put it into the top corner of the net! Yeeeeesss!! It was now 4 - 3 to the Lions! Every single person in an orange seat was up on their feet clapping and cheering wildly. Mr Slake and the Snakes, along with some Scorpions, were looking really annoyed and frustrated. The Lions team piled onto Dover while he laid on his back on the muddy pitch. The Lion's supporters all singing: "IT'S 4-3! ITS 4-3!"

Even though the teachers kept on shouting for everyone to be quiet, no one really cared and kept on singing the same song:

'WE ARE THE CHAMPIONS!

WE ARE THE CHAMPIONS!

NO TIME FOR LOSERS!

'COS WE ARE THE CHAMPIONS, OF THE WORLD!'

The excitement of the Lion's last minute victory stayed with all their supporters for the rest of the afternoon, and when Frank was about to leave and go home, he heard Peter's familiar voice still singing the Lion's song: *'We are the champions'*.

"Frank, wait!" Peter then stopped singing and shouted to him, he must've run really fast because he was panting and had sweat dripping down from his hair.

"I need to tell you something, something important!" Peter said.

As Frank and Peter walked out of the building they saw Lucy walking down the ramp. Peter ran towards her and Frank could hear Peter saying to her the exact same thing he had just told him. They both started to walk towards Frank. Nobody spoke until they got out of the school grounds and alone. Lucy was the first of the trio to actually speak.

"So what's the very important thing you have to tell us about?"

"Do you know the legend of the Enchanted Stone?" Peter whispered.

Lucy knew what it was but Frank had no idea. Peter told him the story: "There was once an ordinary man called Harold Newt in the seventeenth century. One day when he was going to work through the local woods and some goblins appeared from nowhere and attacked him. They took him back to their cave, which is supposedly underneath Severors school. They dropped him into a cauldron of Goblin sweat and blood and he turned into a goblin. Goblins live forever unless you kill them in a special way, so that's why some are about five million years old. Even though Harold was the youngest Goblin, for some reason they made him the King Goblin, and he is now known by the name of Natas Snilbog. He killed every goblin and human that annoyed him in anyway at all. He chopped their heads off, burned them, stabbed them or even chucked them in the dungeons, which is also under the school, to starve. One day, a human discovered the cave and slaughtered Natas Snilbog. When the King Goblin died, he split his soul into eight parts and one of the parts was the person that killed him. No one knows who killed him. There are seven more things that have a part of his soul in them, apart from that, but I can't remember them. One day the King Goblin will be remade in the cave and the first human that he sees will be the last part of his soul, so for him to die, the objects must be destroyed. So, yeh, back to the thing I have to tell you. Snilbog also had a son and he's a vampire and when he dies, his ashes will fuse together and make a stone. That's a part of his soul."

"What, that's the thing you have to tell us?" Lucy asked.

"No, yes, well in my class of Mysteries and Legends, Miss Gaton told us the story again and every time she said, 'Enchanted Stone', Sam Matthews kept making weird noises. Like whimpering, so I think that Sam is the stone," Peter answered.

Lucy burst out laughing, "So *you* think that he's *a vampire*?"

Frank said, "You've no evidence of that Peter!"

"That's where you're wrong Frank. At the house ceremony the other week, when Sam got up, sunlight shone upon him and he was whimpering then," Peter explained.

Lucy stopped laughing, "But when vampires are exposed to sunlight they turn into dust," she said more seriously.

"I think a strong, evil force must've been protecting him - had to be!" Peter said.

Frank decided to change the subject, "Er, where are we walking to?"

"Dunno," Peter said shrugging his shoulders.

They turned around and started to walk back. Frank looked around him, they had wandered onto a train track. Just then he saw that Lucy and Peter were running up a bank, "Come on! Quick Frank!" Peter shouted to him sounding a bit frantic.

He could hear it then and he spun around. A massive steam train had somehow appeared and was racing towards him! It was only about a class room's width away from smashing into him! He noticed the grass on the steep bank that Peter and Lucy had scrabbled up was all wet and slippery so when he leaped onto it he hoped he'd grab something to stop him from slipping back onto the tracks....

He clutched at the wet grass but his hands slid through it and Frank he started to fall backwards. He thought that he would be dead within two seconds, right until something grabbed his hand! Frank could feel the air from the train crash against his leg. He looked up, Peter was there clutching his hand, and Lucy was pulling on Peter's other hand to try to stop him from sliding down the bank, between them they were both desperately trying to drag him up out of danger. But Peter's hand was sweaty and he just couldn't hold him. Frank suddenly knew he wouldn't be able to pull him up!

He started to slide and fall backwards and just when it looked certain he was about to land in front of the train, his jumper snagged on the spiky clump of a small bush and instead of falling onto the track he fell onto the dark coloured wet pebbles right at its side. The train thundered past him so close he could've touched it. Frank finally opened his eyes, he could hardly breathe with the shock of what had just happened.

"ARE YOU CRAZY, FRANK?"

He heard Peter shout as he skidded down the bank to him. Frank lay on his back trying to remember how to breathe while he watched the dark clouds above him moving. Frank closed his eyes, he then opened them to see Peter and Lucy blocking his view of the clouds. Peter gave Frank his red, sweaty hand and pulled him up from the ground. Frank and Peter scrambled together bup the wet, slippery bank while Lucy went up to the path the easy way: up the steps a short distance away. There was an awkward silence when they were all together again walking away from the area.

"Er...thanks for saving me," Frank said, pulling his bag over his right shoulder.

"No problem," Peter said.

"You're welcome," Lucy coughed.

Frank saw it was getting darker by the minute, he suggested that they should start walking home. Lucy took them across a field full of mud and grass. Frank looked up and saw that there were football goals at each end of the field and a muddy white line marking out the pitch.

"Wanna game of footy?" Peter joked.

Chapter 5 - Mr and Mrs Olfankos

Frank finally got home when it was really dark. On the way back Lucy took the long way (on purpose) to a deserted playground. They got a snack from '*OLFANKOS'*, the sweet shop ran by Mr and Mrs Olfanko. The man was called Ravius and normally wore a full black suit. The lady was called Heather, who also wore black. Every time, which is once a year, Frank goes into Olfankos - they always look glum and frustrated. Because Frank had no money, Peter bought him a pack of prawn cocktail crisps.

"I probably wouldn't've bought that, Peter," Frank heard Lucy say as he walked out and she saw the big lolly he'd bought for himself.

He found a rock outside the old shop and sat on it. When Lucy had eaten her *MR ENTO'S FANTASTICALLY FRUITY FLAVOURED SCRUMPTIOUS CHOCOLATE* and Frank had finished his crisps, Peter was still sucking his *BANANA, STRAWBERRY, LEMON, APPLE AND ORANGE LOLLY*. It took him almost half an hour to eat the enormous thing! Peter looked at the lolly wrapper, he started panting and making weird noises and screamed at the top of his lungs: "MY

TEETH! MY TEETH! WHAT COLOUR ARE MY TEETH?"

"My God Peter! Shut Up!" Frank said, which shut Peter up.

"What are my teeth like?" he trembled.

He gave Frank a big smile so he could see his colourful teeth. Peter's teeth had turned orange, green, red and yellow, all the ingredients of the lolly.

"And that's why there's a full jar of them still, because no one has them!" Lucy yawned with a 'I told you so' look on her face.

Frank couldn't hold it in, he erupted into raucous laughter. It took him about thirty seconds to catch his breath. Frank grabbed the wrapper, it said: *WARNING! YOU MAY HAVE COLOURFUL TEETH AFTER EATING THIS.* After that, Peter was eager to get home. When Peter set off to his home, Lucy set off as well leaving Frank alone in the middle of the street. Frank started to run home (well to his shed) and got there at half-past seven. He'd run across the beach and watched the sun set in the pink sky while the cold, dark gray waves crashed against the wet sea wall and onto him. Frank got into the shed and put his light on. His hand went into his soaking wet blue bag and pulled out his timetable for tomorrow.

He scanned through it and something caught his eye.

1PM COOKING/ TEACHER: MR OLFANKOS JOINED BY MRS OLFANKOS

No, it couldn't be, Frank thought. If Ravius and Heather were teaching him cooking, he wouldn't learn anything! Ravius was what kids called 'bonkers' and Heather was always tripping over whilst either eating a toffee, steak or plum pie. Frank took off his wet clothes and draped them around the shed to dry. He put on his track suit and then sat on his Manchester United bed covers, he had nothing to do, he had done his homework at school, and eaten a banana for his tea a few minutes ago. After twenty minutes of thinking what he could do, one thing came into Frank's blank mind: Natas Snilbog and Grampa Joe's computer. Maybe he could find some information about Snilbog and his goblins on-line?

Frank crawled into the dining room and scanned around for the laptop computer. Grampa Joe had hidden it because Grandma Molly had kept trying to look at what he was doing. Frank saw Grampa Joe's desk and it was behind that - not very well hidden then. He picked it up and ran outside back into the shed. He typed into the search bar: *Natas Snilbog.* The computer took a while to connect to the internet and it came up with lots of different websites. Frank clicked on the top website, *'Natas Snilbog facts'*. Frank went through it, everything Peter told him was there, until it said:

Fact 37:   Snilbog was half vampire so his son was a vampire and one of his lives, what he called Vouscers.

Frank went back into the house to put the computer back in its not-so-well hidden place and got back into the shed. He climbed into bed, turned over and before he knew it, he was asleep.

****

Frank was walking to school in the pouring rain which was hammering down onto his head the following morning. He was drenched when he arrived at school. He got to Mr Anderson's class at ten past eight, having left puddling footprints along the corridors. Mr Anderson did the register and then took the class down the Enchanted Hall. Frank, Peter and Lucy sat down at the Lions table. The walls decorated with the colours, orange, green and brown. Frank turned around to see Mr Cuewant looking at him, a gleaming smile on his face displaying all his white teeth. When everyone had come in and sat down, Mr Cuewant stood up and walked over to the front of the stage.

"Younger people, this is our singing assembly, it's Thursday right?"

A few people giggled but most of the hall was silent.

"Must be losing my memory," he mumbled.

They sang songs like, *'Away in a manager'* and other Christmas carols even though it was September. At the end of assembly, having just dismissed all the children, Mr Cuewant suddenly shouted, *"One Last Thing Children!"*

Everyone stopped and turned around, *"Chop Chop!* Quickly off to your classes now!"* he said with a smile on his face and smacking his hands loudly together.

Frank put his right hand in his pocket, pulled out the scrunched up piece of paper with his timetable on it and took a look at what was next: Science with Mr Solte.

All through the lesson Frank's eyes were fixed on the clock. The lesson went really quickly and before he knew it, it was 10.50 (break time). It was cold outside and still pouring down with rain. The wind was howling and everyone apart from

Frank had a waterproof coat and a hat on. Jack and his two friends, Sadio and Sebastian (Seb for short), kept glancing over at Frank. Jack started to limp towards Frank, following behind was Sadio and Seb. Sadio was from South Africa and a black boy, while Seb was from England.

"Hello, Frank and Fatty," Jack said smirking with his friends.

Who was Fatty? Frank looked to his right, Peter was standing there.

"I'm not called Fatty, Jackie," Peter said while stepping forward.

Jack didn't take that too well, he punched Peter round the face making him fall onto the wet ground and his nose bleed. Before Frank could even look up, Seb had punched him as well.

"Don't mess with me, Sadio or Seb," Jack said looking down at Peter and Frank. "Let's go."

Peter looked at Frank. Frank kicked Sadio round the leg while Peter kicked Seb over. Jack's smile was wiped of his face, he turned around to find Lucy standing there. *WHACK!* Lucy punched Jack onto the floor and watched him crawl away with his friends crying their eyes out. Frank, Peter and Lucy smiled at each other, it didn't last long though because Mr Slake suddenly appeared out of nowhere, grabbed Peter by the arm, and Mrs Rose who had appeared with Slake, caught Lucy and Frank by the scruffs of their necks. The two teachers then proceeded to roughly escort their captives back into the building.

"I've got enough evidence to show Maximus what you've done this time," Mr Slake said pulling a yellow camera out of his mouldy pocket.

Slake and Rose took the trio to Mr Cuewant's office. Before Mr Slake could knock on the old, green door, Mr Cuewant opened it as if he was expecting Frank, Peter and Lucy. "Hello Frank, oh you're joined this time by Lucy, Peter, Mrs Rose and Mr Slake! What mischief have you been doing now?" Mr Cuewant chuckled. "Come in, come in, let's sort it all out!"

After ten minutes of hearing a *totally* different story of what had actually happened, Mr Cuewant said to Mr Slake, "And Luke, have you got any *evidence* this time?" as he crossed his arms tightly over his chest.

"*Yes I have!* I've got three boys that are seriously hurt - and the video of them being seriously assaulted!" Mr Slake snarled with a scowl on his ugly, pale face.

"Can I see the video?" Mr Cuewant asked calmly looking at the bruised and bloody children.

Mr Slake pulled out his pockets to find some tissues and a notebook.

"*Where's my camera?*" he bawled while frantically emptying every pocket on his cloak.

"*Your* camera, Luke. Shadrik has just tripped over it, and he didn't take it too well," Mr Cuewant said while looking out of his little window attached to the door.

Slake swung the door open wide to see Shadrik crunching up a small, yellow camera.

"*WHAT ARE YOU DOING YOU IDIOT?*" Mr Slake bellowed while running out of Mr Cuewant's office.

"Huh? Wha', ya wanna get crunched 'swell idiot?" Shadrik said turning around.

"Shadrik...no," Mr Slake said stepping back a few centimetres in alarm.

Shadrik started huffing and ran towards Mr Slake, who did not hesitate. He turned around and ran back down the corridor. Unfortunately for Mr Slake, Shadrik ran after him. Frank, Peter and Lucy watched Slake and Shadrik until they were both out of sight.

"Come on you lot, get back to your classes," Mr Cuewant said peering through his open doorway.

It was maths' with Mr Slake next so they started walking a little sheepishly towards his classroom.

"What d'you think Shadrik'll do when he finds Slake?" Peter asked.

"Either crush him like he did with the camera or knock 'im out!" Frank laughed smugly.

After maths', which was really annoying because Mr Slake only asked either Frank, Peter or Lucy for the answers to the hardest questions he could think of, like two hundred and sixty-five multiplied by three hundred and forty-three...but finally, the bell rang for lunchtime. Jack, Sadio and Seb kept as far away from Frank, Peter and especially Lucy as possible.

"What's the matter with them?" Peter shouted over the

thunder and lightning.

"Scared of us I reckon," Lucy said coldly narrowing her eyes.

"Psst, Lucy, Peter," Frank said in a whisper.

No one turned around.

"PSSSST, LUCY, PETER!"

"What?" asked Peter moving closer to Frank.

"You know yesterday you said you thought that Sam Matthews was a vampire? His lives are called Vouscers." Frank said, still in a whisper.

"I CAN'T HEAR YOU!" Peter shrieked, even louder than before.

"YOU KNOW YESTERDAY YOU SAID YOU THOUGHT SAM MATTHEWS WAS A VAMPIRE? SNILBOG'S LIVES ARE CALLED VOUSCERS!" Frank bellowed.

The wind was getting stronger and stronger by the second and after seconds later of talking to Peter, Mr Cuewant came out of the cloakroom doors and shouted: "EVERYBODY INSIDE! THE WIND'S TOO STRONG!"

Just then a bin came flying across the playground, tipping all its garbage on Jack, Seb and Sadio.

"QUICKLY INSIDE BEFORE IT BLOWS YOU AWAY!" Mr Cuewant continued to shout.

When everyone had got inside, it was one o'clock: Mr and Mrs Olfankos's lesson. Cooking was Frank's least favourite subject, he burnt his fingers every time he cooked something.

When Frank got to the class, everyone was waiting silently and patiently, all excited for the lesson ahead. There were brightly coloured tables with two seats next to each one. Frank sat on a green seat at the front next to Peter's yellow seat, behind Jack and Sadio. The door opened and was then slammed shut a few moments later.

"Good afternoon," Mr Olfankos had moved swiftly to stand in front of the whiteboard. "If you don't know who I am, I am Mr Olfankos and this is Mrs Olfankos, you can call her Heather if you like." he said pointing towards the back of the room, where Heather was sitting in a small red chair eating a toffee and steak pie.

He then said: "I am your new cooking teacher if you didn't know, Cuewant has let me teach you until I decide to leave so I expect you to work hard, cook hard and listen hard. In my opinion, cooking is the fourth most important subject. First is maths, second, literacy, third PE and fourth, cooking. *You will* get here on time or you'll have detention. *You will* do your homework as well, and *you'll ALL,* including Mr Gale and Miss Henrik, *stop sending love letters!*"

Everyone turned around to see Richard Gale passing a small note to Olivia Henrik.

"*PUGI!* Pass me it," Mr Olfankos ordered Peter looking at him sternly.

"Me?" Peter asked looking around the room, perplexed.

"That's your name, Isn't it?"

"Well, no, it's actually *Puginic,*" Peter corrected him.

"I don't care what your name is! To me, you'll always be 'Pugi', NOW SHUT IT!" barked Mr Olfankos.

Peter stood up and walked with a slow shuffle towards Richard. He took the clean, folded up piece of paper out of his hand and passed it to Mr Olfankos.

"'*Meet me in the playground after school, Livvy.'*" he

taunted. "Well, Livvy, if I were you then I wouldn't wait for yeh boyfriend because he's getting double detention after school for not listening during my cooking class!" Mr Olfankos bellowed. "Now...onto the lesson, this term we will be making pizzas."

A few people muttered 'yes' or 'get in there', but Mr Olfankos soon put a stop to that.

"SHUT IT!" he shouted. "Heather, would you mind passing them pens next to you?"

Heather stood up, both of her hands filled with pie and pens and she walked briskly over to her husband. A boy sat at the table in the centre of the room had left his bag in the middle of the walkway between the desks. Heather, not knowing that the bag was there, tripped over it and her toffee and steak pie flew out of her sticky hands right towards Frank. Frank ducked his head down to his knees and as he watched the pie fly over his head, Jack turned his head and got splattered in the face with the pie.

"IT STINGS! IT STINGS! MY EYES HAVE BEEN SET ON FIRE!" he screeched holding his eyes.

Frank could only see a few strands of Jack's brown hair as it was now a brownish yellow and had thick and mushy bits of steak in it. Just then, the bell rang and everyone left the classroom, leaving Mr Olfankos, Heather, Jack and Sadio alone in the room.

"COME TO ME OFFICE AFTER SCHOOL RICHARD!" he shouted as everyone ran out of the classroom.

When they were as far away from Mr Olfankos as possible, everyone erupted into raucous laugher. A lot of people did impressions of Jack, "MY EYES! MY EYES!" They cried while clutching their eyes.

Frank looked down at his timetable, it was art again, unfortunately with Mrs Rose. Frank ran away from the crowd to get there early, he didn't want to be late to his 'most important subject' or get detention. He got to the art class and walked in nonchalantly. Mrs Rose was sitting at her desk writing something, *"SIT, FRANK,"* she snarled.

She was wearing a banana yellow jacket, a crocodile green dress over black trousers.

Even after he had sat down, everyone else was still doing

impressions of Jack, who then came into the classroom.

"SIT!" Mrs Rose shouted.

All the children sat down immediately.

"Today you shall sit in silence and draw something to do with school. Finish it before twenty-five past two or you'll get detention. If you talk you will also get detention." she said calmly looking towards Frank. "Do I make myself clear?"

The classroom was silent. She brought her voice up and shouted, "DO I MAKE MYSELF CLEAR?"

"Yes, Miss," Frank and his classmates said as if they were robots.

Mrs Rose didn't say anything, "You'll sit still and in silence for ten minutes," she whispered.

"What, Why? Miss, I thought you said art was our most important..." Frank stopped.

He knew what he had done. "Double detention for Frank. Why you may ask? It's for talking when it's silence and for calling me Miss, after school detention Frank. I don't care what you're doing after school, you're coming." said Mrs Rose.

Of course, Frank would just sit in his shed when he got home and do his homework. After ten minutes of silence there was still another forty-five minutes of silence to go.

"Frank, collect all the drawings in," she commanded him to do.

The bell rang to signal the end of school and work, well not for Frank, but everyone else ran out of the room. "Frank, my office now, I'll come back in a minute," she said glancing towards her office.

Frank opened the black door and sat down. The walls were coloured yellow and red. He looked around the room, there were pictures of kittens, dogs, flowers and other animals. Above a door in the far corner he saw a small, dirty window but instead of seeing outside, he saw mainly darkness but with a bit of light moving in it. Just then a shape in the window started to move, it was something small and looked circular. Curious, he stood up and walked towards the door; he wasn't tall enough to see what was in there so he got a stool. He could now just make out what was in there. It was a dark, shadowy room with hardly anything in it, except for a figure standing in the middle of this mysterious place. Frank felt his jaw drop and his eyes widen: it was Mrs Rose looking up at Frank!

Startled, Frank heard her voice saying, *"Being nosy are we?"* But it came from behind him! Mrs Rose had silently crept up behind him and was now standing quite unnervingly very close to him. She then kicked the stool making Frank fall onto the stubbly carpet. "SIT!" she barked.

Frank sat down immediately, the chair was uncomfortable and too big so Frank's feet couldn't touch the floor. "Now Frank, you've been in detention a lot recently haven't you?" she said smiling sinisterly. "How can we change that, Frank?" Before Frank could answer Mrs Rose was speaking again. "Why don't you stop arguing with teachers and just be early to your classes?" she sighed in exasperation. "Now, write *'I mustn't speak when it's silence'*, shall we say...ohhh let's say five hundred times?"

Frank couldn't concentrate properly when he started to write *'I mustn't speak when it's silence'* after seeing what seemed to be Mrs Rose in the secret room. He kept glancing up towards the dark window. Finally, after completing his tedious task, detention was over. He walked back to his shed slowly and quietly. The waves crashed against the sea wall as he kept replaying in his mind what he'd seen. Had he seen Mrs Rose locked in that darkened room, or had he just imagined he had? But if he hadn't imagined it, who or what was the Mrs. Rose in the art room with him…?

Chapter 6- The Elf Chamber

The weekend went fast as Frank slept through most of it but on Sunday night, it was cold and he tossed and turned around in his bed. He still couldn't stop thinking about what he had seen at detention. If he did see Mrs Rose in the corner, who was teaching art? He finally got to sleep at around one o'clock.

BEEP, BEEP, BEEP! It was cold and windy outside but warmish inside the shed. Frank had a banana for his breakfast and got dressed into his dirty school uniform. He set off to school and as he walked across the beach it started to hailstone. Even though it was hard to see, he could clearly hear when the cold and massive sea waves crashed near by. When Frank finally got to school, his register class was waiting for him.

"Come on Frank, we've been waiting for you!" Mr Anderson said while beckoning Frank to sit down.

Frank sat down behind Henry Holloway and in front of Jack Shaw. Half way through the register something hit Frank on the back of his head. He looked down under his desk, it was a scrunched up piece of paper.

"Psst, *Bullsy*, whatever your name is, *Bullsy*, psst!" Frank turned around, Seb was smirking but Jack had an even bigger smirk on his ugly face.

"What? Telling me how nice that cake was yesterday?" Frank answered; Jack's smile was soon off his face and was now on Frank's.

"No, yeh know that chubby kid and that useless girl, is it Pety and Lucer?" Jack laughed; Frank could feel his fists clenching up.

"What, Lucy that nearly knocked you out and made you and your wimpy friends cry?" Frank taunted back chuckling as he spoke.

Jack and Seb looked at each with sheepish and disgusted faces, "What did you say to me, *Bullsy*?" Jack whispered coldly narrowing his eyes.

"I'm not called *Bullsy*! And I said that you and yeh friends are *wimps!*" Frank said angrily.

"What are you called then, *Bullsy*?" Jack said smirking.

"Frank Burray, *Jackie*," Frank answered Jack.

"*Never...ever...call...me...Jackie!*" Jack said through his teeth.

Luckily, before things escalated any further, erupting into something bad happening, Mr Anderson told everyone to line up at the door.

"Wait, what? I thought it was science at half past - isn't it?" Frank asked the teacher, and with a confused face he pulled out his timetable.

"It's science tomorrow Frank, today it's assembly at half nine."

Mr Anderson led them to the Hall to sit down at their house tables. Once again, Frank and his classmates were the first ones into the Hall. Frank sat in between Peter and Lucy on the opposite side of the room from Jack, Sadio and Seb. Jack kept glancing darkly towards Frank and Peter. After everyone was inside the hall and all the teachers were seated, Mr Cuewant stood up.

"Hello children, today I've only brought you first-years in to talk to you about something." Frank then noticed a few - well a lot of seats were empty and that the Hall was quieter than normal.

"This year, Severors school will be holding a Spelling Bee,

but you'll only be competing against people in your own year group. There will be ten children competing in the Spelling Bee and the winner will get a *wonderful* prize. If you want to participate in this competition, I will leave a sheet of paper on a board next to Mr Slake's classroom. You have forty-eight hours to put your name on the sheet and I will split the children that put their names on the sheet into groups and the top two will go into the competition. The Spelling Bee will take place on Friday, but I will give the participants a spelling practice sheet on Wednesday. Do any of you have any questions?" He asked looking round all the assembled pupils, no one had.

Mr Cuewant then spoke about some other things before letting the children out.

Frank's first lesson was Maths with Slake, so he decided to go and look at the Spelling sheet. When Frank got to Mr Slake's classroom, he realised that a lot of the other children had also got the same idea as he had. Some were putting their name on the sheet, others were just staring at it and others were just doing impressions of Jack, still. Frank made a determined attempt to look at the piece of paper. He pushed through the crowd, knocking four or five kids over, and eventually got to the front. A single sheet of A4 paper was on the board saying:

SPELLING BEE - ENTER YOUR NAME HERE.

There were already some names scrawled on the sheet: *Gary Davis, Harry Simpson, Holly Griffin.* Frank counted about a dozen as he scanned down it before five names stood out from all the rest. They were, *Lucy Dart, Peter Puginic, Jack Shaw, Seb Nelson and Sadio Lasogga.* Seeing that Peter's and Lucy's names were on it he decided he'd put his name on as well. A girl pushed in front of him and wrote her name: 'Emma Parkinson', on it, then Frank wrote his name down. When he got out of the crowd of kids he met Lucy and Peter at Slake's door.

"You put your name on yet Frank?" Peter asked him.

"Just done it – I saw you two put your names on as well."

An unpleasant voice then interrupted them. "You lot put your names down to spell 'Hello'? Or are you just trying to humiliate each other?"

Frank turned around to see Jack followed closely by Seb and Sadio.

"About to ask you the same thing, Jackie," Peter said stepping forward to confront him.

"Thought I told yeh to stop calling me Jackie, Petty?" Jack said narrowing his brown eyes.

" - Least I'm not the one that's getting laughed at for nearly crying when a cake goes in my face," Peter said also narrowing his eyes.

Just then the bell rang.

"You lot won't even get into the competition!" Jack shouted while running down the corridor to his next class.

Frank, Peter and Lucy walked into maths to find Mr Slake standing only about a metre away from the door. "There are names on the desks, *you'll* sit there today." he said with an evil smile on his face.

There were three rows of eight seats, Frank's seat was in the corner at the back of the room, Lucy at the opposite corner and Peter was directly in the middle at the front.

"Burray, swap with Puginic: I want to keep an eye on *you* today." Mr Slake said smirking. "You'll be doing a test today, there are forty-four questions and a possible mark of fifty. I expect you all to get over thirty-eight marks, you have forty-five minutes, don't start until I say, and Burray will now hand them out - try not to miss giving one to anybody." He said sarcastically.

The first half an hour went really quickly and before Frank knew it, the forty-five minutes was up.

"Now everyone out and go to your next class...GET OUT NOW!" Mr Slake bellowed while opening the door.

Looking at the Spelling Bee entry sheet as he passed it, Frank saw that not many people had put their names down after his. Next it was history with Mr Feather, a man who had a long moustache and was around sixty years old. History was on the other side of the school from mathematics so he decided to quickly get away from everyone - and not run - because it was most likely he would get stopped by Shadrik or another teacher. So he speed-walked along the long corridors to Mr Feather's classroom. Surprisingly, not one teacher he'd passed on the way stopped him and he got to his class on time; Frank had a bad habit of getting stopped by teachers on the way to his next class, when that happened he'd be late and get a detention.

Mr Feather was sat at his desk when Frank walked in, "Hello Frank, take a seat." he said with a smile on his face.

Mr Feather was one of the few teachers that Frank hadn't argued with or got shouted at by. Frank didn't really like history but he listened all through the lesson about how King Henry VIII had six wives, beheaded two of them when he got fed up with them, and killed lots of other people as well, but got away with all of that because he was the King.

At lunchtime it was snowing and by half-past two the snow was so deep that the teachers' cars were buried upto their windows.

At home-time Mr Cuewant was at the school gates saying, 'get home safely' to everyone as the children trudged past him through the deep snow. Most of them in were in groups, one of those groups was Frank, Peter and Lucy. They said that they'd go to what kids called, '*The Haunted Forest*' and have a snowball fight. Frank had his Manchester United scarf on and a blue, warm woolly coat on. After twenty minutes of struggling through the snow and falling over a lot, they finally got to the forest. The trees were heavily covered in snow and the snow on the ground was the thickest Frank had ever seen in his life.

"I can't believe how much – *Ouch!* What was that?" Frank said turning around rubbing the back of his head.

Jack, Seb and Sadio were standing about a classroom's length away from them. "Well well well…Hello Frank, and I see you're with your little friends, mmm, it maybe harder than we expected," Jack said, his hands behind his back.

"What you talking about Jack*ie*?" Frank asked not moving a muscle.

"Hope that scarf still keeps you warm after a few snowballs in your face," Jack said and he then did an overhead throw and a giant snowball came out his hand and flew through the air, just missing Frank's head.

Frank saw that both Seb and Sadio's hands were behind their backs. Frank looked quickly to Peter and Lucy, "GET DOWN ON THE FLOOR!" He bellowed at them.

"FIRE!" Jack shouted at the same time while picking more snow up.

Sadio and Seb threw their snowballs and both hit the targets they'd aimed at: Peter and Lucy. Frank launched a gigantic snowball at Jack and knocked him over into the deep snow. Then Peter threw one, whilst on his knees and upto his waist in the snow, it hit Seb right in the middle of his chest, making him topple over backwards so he was nearly buried in the snow. Lucy, instead of throwing hers from a distance ran as close as she could to Sadio and threw a massive snowball with all of her power at him. It had so much power in it it made him do several backward roly-poly flips until he hit a tree and a huge load of heavy snow fell onto him!

There were snowballs flying everywhere, big ones, small ones, rock-solid ones and worst of all, wet and mushy ones which went down their t-shirts and made them even wetter and colder. Then Frank launched another enormous snowball which made Sadio fall over backwards again, Jack threw one at Peter but miraculously Lucy threw another snowball and hit Jack's making it explode into tiny pieces. Frank then threw another snowball he'd really packed hard first, and it hit Jack right in the middle of his forehead, making him whinge and wail as he went down on his knees. Jack and Sadio were now crawling away in retreat, leaving Seb alone with the three of them. Seb knew that he wouldn't have a chance of beating all three of them so he ran to Jack and Sadio, dragged them up onto their feet, and they staggered together out of the forest, well and truly defeated!

Frank, Peter and Lucy all sat in the snow on the forest floor exhausted. Their three enemies were now out of sight. "Stupid – Snakes - I need to - catch my - breath." Lucy panted while watching to making sure they didn't come back.

Just then, when Frank thought he could relax, he felt a hard snowball whack against his back. "Peter! - Just let me relax for a minute!" Frank moaned.

Then he realised Peter was just a few metres in front of him so he assumed it was Lucy, "Lucy, let me relax, just for a minute!"

He then noticed Lucy was about a metre in front of Peter, so who had thrown the snowball? Before Frank could even turn around, three more snowballs were chucked at his head. He then noticed that Peter and Lucy were being pelted as well!

"It's those stupid idiot Snakes, JUST LEAVE US ALONE!" Frank shouted as he turned around.

He was expecting to see that Jack and his two henchmen had circled behind them but instead he saw dozens of small, hooded creatures....

"What the hell? Er... Peter, Lucy?" Frank said looking over his shoulder; Peter and Lucy had also noticed the mysterious creatures.

"What are they?!" asked Peter.

"Not a clue," Lucy said.

The creatures then took their hoods down. They all had long noses with big round protruding eyeballs that looked like footballs. "HUMANS!" squeaked one of the little creatures with an especially long nose.

"Mr Man, Mr Other Man, Miss Lady. *I'm Teethy the Elf!*" It said looking up at Frank, Peter and Lucy; Teethy had teeth that were bigger than his fingers and looked like he didn't stop cleaning them, every inch of every tooth was sparkling white.

"Mr Sir. Miss Madame, what do people name you?"

"Are you...er...Elves?" Frank asked.

"We are Elves, are you humans?" asked an Elf at the back

staring at them with his big, brown eyes.

"Yes, we are, it's very nice to meet you," Lucy said trying desperately to think what to say whilst shaking Teethy's hand.

"What do other humans call you humans?" shouted an Elf at the front looking up at Peter like he was a giant.

"My name's Frank, this is Lucy and this is Peter," Frank said bending down. "What are your names?"

The Elves went silent, "What - are - our - names?" an Elf asked while his eyes widened.

"Mr humans have never asked Elves what names they have!" another Elf gasped, his eyes also widening.

Then lots of different elves started to shake each of Frank's, Peter's and Lucy's hands. Lots of different names were flying at all three of the kids: 'Dodgy', Apple', 'Yosh', 'Inky', 'Curty', 'Dobb', 'Nolet', 'Suver', all of the Elves kept wanting to shake their hands. "Master might like you humans," said Teethy. Frank was curious to find out who 'Master' was.

"Who is 'Master'?" Frank asked him.

The Elf who had said his name was 'Apple' looked at the

other Elves who all vigorously nodded their heads at the same time as if they were agreeing to an unspoken question

"Would you and your friends like to meet Master, Mr Frank?" asked Apple.

"OK, where does Master live?" Frank asked curiously.

"Master lives in the Elf Chamber," Nolet said.

"Do you really want to see Master, humans?" Dodgy asked.

Frank turned around looking for suggestions from Peter or Lucy.

"Why not?" shrugged Peter.

"Yeh, sure," Frank said. Suddenly all the Elves started to pull Frank, Peter and Lucy into the forest. "Ummmmm, Teethy, where are you taking us?" Frank asked.

"The Elf Chamber, Mr Frank," Teethy answered.

The Elves took Frank, Peter and Lucy through the giant trees and in a large , frozen, muddy hole. Then Teethy told Frank, "We all have to say: *'Eht enots, eht enots, sah ot eb deyortsed ni fle rebmahc, ni eht dnomaid rafknot, Snilbog nos,'* to open the Elf Chamber."

Then Teethy took Frank's hand, Apple took Lucy's and Dodgy took Peter's. All the Elves whispered together what Teethy had just told Frank and one by one they started to fall into the hole – and disappeared! Frank looked at Peter, he was looking at Lucy, who was looking at Apple. She then disappeared into the frozen mud hole with Apple! Peter then looked at Frank with a worried face. Peter was pulled closer to the opening by Dodgy – and then they both disappeared as well! That left Frank with Teethy and only a few other Elves left around the entrance hole. Frank looked at Teethy, he was muttering something, probably the password and then he and Teethy were sucked into the mud. Frank flew down what looked like a dark slide - and he went really fast down it. He couldn't see anything in front of him or behind him, he could feel legs behind him so he assumed that he was in front of Teethy. After ten more seconds Frank was still going down, he finally reached the bottom and flew out of the slide with a big thump. Shortly after, Teethy flew out of the slide. Frank couldn't believe what he was seeing, there was a huge tunnel with bright lights changing colours every few seconds. Frank looked behind him again, the slide that he had just flew down was not there anymore - he just saw a brick wall!

"Teethy, where's the slide gone?" Frank asked still trying to see a bit of the slide.

"Back to the entrance, Mr Frank" Teethy squeaked.

"How do we get back out again?" Frank said.

"Say the special words again, and the slide with come down and pick Mr Frank, Mr Peter and Miss Lucy to slide back up," Teethy explained.

Teethy then grabbed Frank's hand and started to walk down the tunnel. "Is this The Elf Chamber?" Frank asked looking curiously at the now green lights.

"No, no, no! This is the actual entrance to the Elf Chamber, Mr Frank." Teethy answered.

The tunnel was really long and actually quite hot. Frank and Teethy got to the end of the tunnel after about two minutes of walking, and when Frank saw what the Elf Chamber looked like, his jaw dropped.

It was like a cave, with hundreds of little Elves all walking around with clothes, food and other objects in barrels. There were Elves with long noses, Elves with tennis ball-sized eyes and most of the Elves wore a jumper which was too big for them. An Elf, with a long fat nose, walked over to Frank.

"Hello Mr Human, what Elves call me is Parry the Elf, what do humans call you? Would you like some food?" The Elf asked while handing him a mince pie.

"I'm called Frank, Parry," Frank said starting on his mince pie.

"PARRY, TALK TO MR FRANK LATER!" Teethy shouted.

"Fine, bye, Mr Frank," Parry said handing him three more mince pies.

"Would you like to meet Master, Mr Frank?" Teethy asked.

"Yeh, OK, where does 'Master' live?" Frank asked.

"The Elf Tower where everyone sleeps, Mr Frank." Teethy said. "Teethy lives there as well Mr Frank, Teethy lives at the top of The Elf Tower, Teethy will show Mr Frank Teethy's room, when Mr Frank meets Master."

Teethy took Frank's hand and led him towards a door at the other end of the chamber, Frank looked around, there were hundreds and hundreds of Elves, all tiny and carrying something, and going somewhere with it, they all looked very intent on doing - whatever it was they were doing!

There were steps leading up to what looked like scaffolding that went really high up. Frank then noticed somebody that caught his eye, it was Peter! He was up on the highest part of the cave looking through a half open door and waving to him!

"Does Mr Frank want to see our special rooms?" Teethy asked looking up at Frank.

"Yeh, OK," Frank said.

"Would Mr Frank like to see Elves' Kitchen?" Teethy asked scratching his forehead.

"Yeh OK, where's the kitchen, Teethy?" Frank asked.

Teethy took Frank's hand and took him down some steps into a dark corridor. There were small, open doors on each side all the way down the corridor. While Teethy took Frank down the corridor, the boy glanced at what was inside the mysterious rooms. There were signs on the doors saying things like, *SCIENCE ROOM* and *SPORTS ROOM*, inside the Sports Room there were some Elves playing tennis and some playing basketball. Finally Teethy stopped at the *COOKING ROOM*.

Teethy opened the red door and Frank saw hundreds of Elves in there with aprons on. Inside the kitchen it smelt like apple pie with cream and custard! - It smelt like Yorkshire puddings with gravy as well!

"What's for dinner tonight, Yoville?" Teethy asked a small Elf standing next to a massive oven and stove.

"Spaghetti, pizza, Yorkshire puddings, chicken, beef, gravy, carrots, broccoli and for pudding, apple pie, ice-cream, chocolate cake, chocolate, fudge and banana ice cream." Yoville said.

"OK, Yoville! Nice one! Thanks Yoville." Teethy said.

"Would you like to stay for dinner, Mr Frank?"

Frank had his answer ready, and with his mouth watering he quickly said: "Yes! Please Teethy!"

"Would Mr Frank like to meet Master now?" Teethy asked.

"Yeh, OK," said Frank.

Teethy took his hand and walked him up the steps made out of shiny stones. When Frank got to the top of the stairs he was relieved to find his friends Peter and Lucy waiting for him.

"Hi Frank," Peter said nonchalantly. But Lucy stated excitedly, *"This Is Amazing, isn't it?"*

"It certainly is Lucy! Are you both staying for dinner as well?" Frank asked them.

"OH Yeh! Deffo!" They both said at the same time.

"We're off to 'The Elf Tower', are you?" Peter asked.

"Yeh," Frank said.

Teethy, Apple and Dodgy took them to a really tall building, the size of Big Ben in London, and opened a giant door. There were hundreds of steps leading up and every few steps there was a door with a number on.

"Teethy lives at room seven nine two, near the top." Teethy said. "Dodgy lives at room five eight six and Apple lives at room three three four. Master lives at eight zero zero, the highest room."

After five minutes of walking, they were up to room seven six eight. "This is a long way up isn't it?" Peter said panting loudly, "My legs are aching!"

"Yeh, yeh it is, mine too! I'm nearly done in…!" Frank

panted back. Lucy though seemed quite unaffected by the climb so far, and said bossily to them, "C'mon! C'mon! Hurry up you two - and stop moaning!"

When they finally got to the top they were all sweating and panting, but Lucy wasn't as much as the two boys were though.

"How come you lot aren't tired and sweating?" Frank asked the Elves looking at their dry faces.

"Elves have got used to going up and down The Elf Tower and so we don't get tired by it, Mr Frank!" Teethy said.

'Master's' door was made out of wood and was really big. Teethy knocked on the door three times and as the knocks were echoing around them the door slightly opened.

"Who is it?" came a whisper from inside.

"Teethy, Dodgy and Apple, Master. We've got humans, Master. Can we come in Master?" Teethy asked.

"Yes, OK, Teethy," the voice said, a bit louder this time.

Teethy opened the creaky door, there was a bed, a bathroom, a chest of drawers with different coloured drawer fronts, and a big, red rocking chair in the middle of the room with, what looked like an ancient fossil of a creature sitting on it. But it wasn't a fossil it was an ancient looking, larger Elf than the others. He had small glasses perched on his long pointy nose.

"Mmmm...Humans," the ancient Elf croaked. "Humans, I'm called Sodonpo Frangini, Teethy has probably told you I'm called Master but you can call me Frangini, ummmmmm... Mr...?"

"Frank, Peter and Lucy," Frank said pointing at the person when he said their name.

"Teethy was wondering, Master, if Master wanted to meet Mr Frank and Mr Peter and Miss Lucy and Teethy was wondering if Master wanted to have dinner with Mr Frank and Mr Peter and Miss Lucy." Teethy said on his knees.

"Oh do Stand Up, Teethy! I might be your Master but I'm not King Goblin- no -King Elf." Frangini said.

Teethy's smile was wiped off his face and he cried out, "No! You're certainly not King Goblin- King Goblin is the one that Teethy doesn't like or respect- Teethy was made sad by the King Goblin when he was young- but King Goblin died and so Teethy is happy now! - Teethy likes his new Master- King

Goblin was bad- Teethy needs to go now- goodbye Master- oh I'm not going like forever Master! - Master protects his Elves- see you at dinner Master! - Goodbye Mr Frank and Mr Peter and Miss Lucy!" And he ran out of the room sobbing.

"Why has Teethy run off? Have we said something?" Peter asked.

"No, no, don't worry about Teethy, you'll get used to him. So – it seems that you're our guests today?" Frangini said. There was a silence and then Frangini said, "Staying for dinner? The elves must like you as they brought you in, they don't normally tell humans about our chamber, please don't tell anyone else will you? Look, I know you're worrying about Teethy, it's just…his past…he doesn't like me talking about his old master."

"What? Who was his old master? Why did he keep talking about Natas Snilbog… the King Goblin?" Frank asked.

"Do you know the legend, well no, it's actually the true story of King Goblin or as you might call him, Natas Snilbog?" Frangini asked looking at them with his eagle-like eyes.

Frank looked at both Peter and Lucy. "Yeh, well, sort of…"

Frank said nervously.

"Well, as you might of heard, his real name used to be, Harold Newt, well... THAT'S WRONG! HE WAS AN ELF, HIS MUM WAS AN ELF, HIS DAD WAS AN ELF. Sorry! I can get annoyed sometimes, his name was Nutusinkop and... well...he...I used to be his Master...and he just decided...one day...that, well, he probably did the worst thing possible...he went out into the human world, all alone, and the Goblins that lived under the school kidnapped him and well...as you know they turned him into a Goblin and made him their King. He became the most evil Goblin of all time, but Teethy was already a Goblin and when Nutusinkop became King of the Goblins, he was Teethy's master. Just before Nutusinkop disappeared, Teethy became an Elf by drinking a special potion so that's why he's half goblin, half Elf. More Elf though - fortunately!" Frangini said.

"Oh..." Frank just didn't know what else to say.

Frangini looked at his old, dusty watch, "Well it's nearly dinner time, so we'd better go down - shall we?" he said getting up out of his chair, moving quite agilely for such an ancient and wizened looking creature!

Chapter 7- The Elves' Dinner

When Frank, Peter and Lucy went down for dinner, it was seven o'clock.

"Will I get home in time?" Peter asked a small Elf in the middle of the cave.

"What time do you want to get home, Human?" the Elf grunted.

"I don't know…half-seven?" he said.

"You can go home now and we'll get you lots of food to take home?" the Elf said.

Peter looked at Frank and Lucy, "Yeh, I need to get home, my mum will be worried about me," he said to Frank and Lucy.

"HUMAN LEAVING WANTING FOOD!" the Elf shrieked looking down at the steps to the kitchen.

It took less than a minute for a kitchen Elf to come running up to them, staggering a bit, because he had a large heavy sack slung over his shoulder, the Elf said "I filled it full of different kinds of foods for Human to take-away!" Peter thanked the Elf and taking the sack off him he swung it over his shoulder – and he noticed it was quite heavy even for him!

"Will you take Human to his house through the *The Tunnel Of Elf Chamber*?" The Elf then asked all the other Elves around them.

One Elf took hold of Peter's free hand and they all ran towards a round entrance into a dark tunnel.

"See you tomorrow!" Peter shouted trying to keep up with the Elves and waving at the same time.

"Can I go too? I need to get home, sorry Elves, and Frank," Lucy then said.

"ANOTHER HUMAN LEAVING AND WANTING FOOD!" The Elf shrieked again.

Once again, the same Elf as before soon came staggering up from the kitchen with a sack full of food!

"Take this Human to her house through The Tunnel of Elf Chamber as well." The Elf said not even looking up at them.

An Elf took Lucy's free hand and started to run like they did with Peter. When Lucy was out of sight, Frangini came out of the stairs leading up to his room.

"Where've your friends gone, Mr Frank?" Frangini asked looking around him.

"They've gone home, I'm here though," Frank said.

"Oh good, good." Frangini said walking over to Frank. Then he turned and shouted, "START THE TABLE, ELVES!"

Just then, Teethy came down the old, spiral staircase and looked like he was out of breath.

"Sorry Master, Teethy is a bit late,"

"It's alright Teethy just go and join in the table making," Frangini said.

"Sorry Master," he repeated, "Oh, hello Mr Frank," and he ran off to where the other Elves were.

Then Frank turned around. Amazed, his jaw dropped. The Elves all had three different colour blocks of foam in their hands and were making a long table. Some bits of foam were used as the chairs and some were shaped for the table.

"How do they know how to make it?" Frank asked Frangini.

"Practice, lots and lots of practice." he answered.

Frank stood there in silence for a few moments and just watched the Elves make the table.

"Incredible, isn't it?" Frangini said watching them.

Frank tried to say 'Yes!' but when he opened his mouth nothing came out. After they were finished, every single Elf, except Frangini, went running into the kitchen. After a few moments of silence, the murmurs of Elves down the corridor got louder and louder. Then every Elf that came back into the main bit of the cave had both of their little hands carrying large plates full with all sorts of food. Chicken, Spaghetti, Pizza, Chips, nearly everything you could think of eating for dinner was either piled up on the Elves' plates or on the long, squishy table. Then Frangini, without warning shouted, "SIT! Frank, you sit next to my chair, you see that there's two big chairs, you sit next to the one that's right at the end of the table."

Frank sat down in the red, comfy chair, next to Teethy.

"Are you alright?" Frank asked Teethy.

"Yes Mr Frank, Teethy is alright," he answered.

Then Frangini walked over to his big, yellow chair and stood in front of it. "HELLO ELVES!" He had to shout for the elves at the other end of the table to hear him. "THIS LOOKS REALLY NICE SO THANK YOU FOR MAKING THIS DINNER TONIGHT. LET THE FEAST…" there was a silence then he shouted…"*BEGIN!*"

Frank filled his plate with sausages, noodles, spaghetti, pizza and some bits of chicken. He then got some water and poured it into his glass. He didn't know where to begin.

"Come on Mr Frank eat up, you're not in Fairyland, so it's quite safe to eat in here!" Teethy said putting a bit of sausage into his mouth. Seeing Frank's puzzled look he explained, "I mean if Mr Frank ate some food in Fairyland he'd never be able to leave because Fairies put magic stuff into it. But we don't! Mr Frank can go away and come back when he likes!"

Frank muttered, "Oh, er, thank you Teethy..." He then got a big slice of pizza and put it into his mouth. The food smelt and tasted really nice to him – compared to the usual scavenged banana, apple or old leftovers he normally got to eat - and he was soon on his third plateful of sausage pizza. After about forty five minutes of non-stop eating, Frangini stood up again, "TIME FOR PUDDING!" he shouted.

Then just like they did before, every single Elf except Frangini, ran back into the kitchen and when they came back out this time they had bowls filled with all different kinds of puddings. There was Apple pie, custard, brownies, chocolate, fudge, chocolate and toffee cake, ice cream, biscuits and sour sweets. Once again, after everyone had sat back down, Frangini stood up and bellowed, *"BEGIN!"*

Frank got a variety of things on his plate, Apple pie and custard, brownies, fudge and cake. The Apple pie was warm and had big, crunchy bits of apple in it and the brownies, fudge and cake all were delicious as well. After twenty minutes of talking to Teethy and Frangini, between mouthfuls of puddings, about all the things that are happening in the world, Frangini's jaw dropped when he found out there has been World War Two and that the year was 2018 not 1903 like he thought it was!

Frangini then finally stood up for the third, and last time of the night and shouted, "THANK YOU ELVES FOR THIS WONDERFUL FEAST TONIGHT! IT'S NOW TIME FOR BED! GOODNIGHT EVERYONE!"

Frank decided to ask Frangini if he was allowed to go home.

"Yes, of course - TEETHY! Before you go to bed, will you take Mr Frank to his house, through The Tunnel of Elf Chamber?" Frangini asked Teethy.

"Yes Master," Teethy said taking Frank's hand. "Come on Mr Frank," he said, starting to run.

Frank ran with him but Teethy suddenly stopped at the part where Peter and Lucy had gone through. "The Tunnel Elves have locked all entrances and locked all exits, Mr Frank, you can't leave until seven o'clock tomorrow morning, Mr Frank. You'll have to sleep here tonight Mr Frank," Teethy said scratching his forehead.

Frank couldn't believe his ears! *Here? He had to sleep here?*

"Master, please will you come to the entrance of The Tunnel of Elf Chamber?" Teethy shouted.

Frangini came down the spiral staircase and walked towards Frank. "What's the matter, Teethy?" he asked.

"Master! Master! The Tunnel Elves had shut the entrances and the exits when Teethy and Mr Frank went to go home!" Teethy whimpered, now very upset.

"Teethy, it's OK! Stop fretting" Frangini told him. "And for you Frank, Teethy's right, you'll have to sleep here. ELVES, WAKE UP! HUMAN WANTS A ROOM AND A BED FOAM!"

All the Elves came rushing down the stairs and ran towards the corner where the blocks of foam were. The Elves got a block each and made a layer of foam. They then made another layer, then another until it was like a house and they even left a bit of room for the door. Then half a dozen Elves went into the green house and formed a line. Then the Elf who was at the end, next to the blocks of foam, picked up a block and passed it to the next Elf. They kept on doing it for about two minutes and then they all ran up the stairs.

While waiting for them to make the house, Frank saw something at the other end of the cave. It was a largish cupboard and it had a diamond shaped object which looked like it was made out of metal with a small hole inside of it, fastened to the middle of the door, which was partly open. Above it was a gold plaque that had 'TONKFAR' etched into it.

"Frangini, what's that?" Frank asked, pointing to it.

Frangini looked at it, "Oh, that? It's a Tonkfar, Frank," he said, his hands behind his back.

"Oh, er, what is it and what does it do?" Frank asked.

Frangini looked at it, then blankly at Frank with not even a smile on his ancient face. "Teethy, would you please come here and go and close the Tonkfar?" he called out, looking very serious without his usual smile on his face, and he didn't reply to Frank's questions. Frank just shrugged his shoulders and turned away.

Teethy came out of the house and ran towards the Tonkfar, closed it and ran back. After that, the house was ready for him. Frank went inside, it looked amazing! The walls were red and the bed was four layers high, nowhere near the ceiling which was nine layers high, and was yellow.

"Wow! Thank you...I...this...*this is amazing!*" Frank spluttered not knowing what to say.

"COVERS AND PILLOWS!" Frangini shouted.

The Elves immediately ran upstairs, all pushing each other over on the way up. Then they came down the stairs with some... Manchester United covers! Frank was astonished, "How did they know?" he asked Frangini who was now smiling again.

Frangini did not answer, he only winked at Frank. Then another few Elves came down the stairs with two pillows in their hands. When they were finished, Frank got into his bouncy bed. He looked out of the window at the Tonkfar.

"Go to sleep as soon as the lights go out, and one more rule Mr Frank, don't go out of this room after dark. Goodnight!" Frangini said walking out of the house.

"*LIGHTS OUT!*" he shouted and everything went black.

Frank could just make out the Tonkfar as his eyes adjusted to the dark because it seemed to glow round the edges just a little bit, and he went to sleep watching it.

Frank woke up at six-thirty, he hadn't woken up once through the night as his bed was so comfy. He put his orange shirt and black trousers on for school. He then got back into the warm and comfy bed for a bit as everything was quiet and the Elves weren't up yet. But thirty seconds later loads of Elves ran down the stairs and towards Frank's house, shouting: "WAKEY WAKEY MR FRANK!" Teethy's giant eyes were only about a centimetre away from Frank's when he opened his eyes.

"OK, OK! I'll get up!" Frank groaned rubbing his eyes.

When Frank went out of his little house, he immediately saw that the long foam table was almost overflowing with bacon, eggs, beans, scrambled eggs, sausages, tomatoes, toast, pancakes, cereals, anything you could think of for having at breakfast! Frangini walked down the stairs with his long, grey hair all mussed up and in his eyes and over his small glasses. His grey moustache was messy and untidy as he walked over to Frank, "Morning, Frank," Frangini yawned, his eyes opening and closing. "Staying...for...sorry, I'm a bit tired...are you staying for breakfast, Mr Frank?"

"What? Oh Yes! Look at all this!" Frank said his eyes wide.

"ELVES...IT'S...TIME FOR...BREAKFAST...*SIT!* Frank, you... sit where you sat last night." Frangini said pointing towards the red chair he'd sat in the night before.

Frank looked back at his foam house but all he saw was dirt and rocks sticking out of the walls!

"YOU MAY BEGIN FEASTING!" Frangini shouted, his voice echoing across the room.

Frank looked at his watch, it was a quarter to seven. Then he got two thick pieces of toast, eggs, some sausages and a few pieces of bacon and made a sausage, bacon and egg sandwich. After breakfast, Frank started to walk to the slides as it was a quarter to eight but he was stopped by Teethy. "MR FRANK! MR FRANK! WHERE IS MR FRANK GOING?" He squeaked running after him.

"I'm going to school," Frank said.

"NO! Teethy will take Mr Frank to school through the The Tunnel of Elf Chamber!" he said.

"Oh, OK." Frank replied and they went together into The Tunnel of Elf Chamber.

The tunnel was dark and after about five minutes of walking Teethy stopped. The Elf gave Frank an old piece of paper and whispered looking around them to make sure no one was eavesdropping, "It's the secret password for the Elf Chamber if you would like to come again Mr Frank!"

Frank thanked him, and leaned down putting his arm out to shake his hand, which surprised Teethy because he didn't know what to do with it! Frank then walked away, but kept looking back at his new little friend, waving goodbye to him. Teethy waved goodbye back to him with a big happy smile on his face. Frank suddenly felt himself getting sucked into what seemed

107

like a pipe. Then, before he knew it, he was in a toilet cubicle, and on opening the door he found himself inside a familiar looking boys' toilets. He cautiously walked to the exit door and looked out along the corridor - he was inside Severors Secondary School!

Chapter 8- Mr Slake's Detention

Frank walked slowly down the corridor, and looked in the cloakrooms, they were silent and empty, but just then he heard footsteps coming up the corridor so he retraced his steps to find somewhere to hide from whomever was coming. The footsteps were getting louder and louder, then they were right next to him.

"YOU!" A man shouted at him, grabbing his arm and pulling him out of the cloakrooms into the corridor. It was Mr Slake standing in front of him, Frank couldn't see all of his face, because his black, mouldy cape's hood was covering up most of it. Frank knew where he was going to take him; Mr Cuewant's office…Mr Slake dragged him along the floor until he was standing outside the office.

"Get - In," he muttered menacingly whilst knocking on the door.

"Come in, Luke," Frank heard a voice cheerfully say from inside.

Slake beckoned him to stand up and open the door, then pushed him in.

Mr Cuewant was sitting in his swingy chair, his hands folded on the wooden table top.

"Hello, Luke, and what are you doing here so early Frank?" he said with a small grin under his beard as he winked at Frank.

"This child has climbed over the fence and - "

"THAT IS NOT TRUE!" Frank interrupted Mr Slake.

"Yes it is you Liar! You know that it's True! How else would you get into the school?!" Mr Slake said fiercely.

"Luke, would you leave me and Mr Burray here alone so we can sort out what has happened?" Mr Cuewant said calmly.

Slake did not answer, he just huffed loudly, narrowed his eyes and stomped out of the room.

"Mr Cuewant...that is not true...I didn't do that...I...Well I had...you may not believe this but...I had dinner and breakfast with..." Frank was interrupted by Mr Cuewant.

"Elves?" he said calmly.

"What?!...*How did you know?*" Frank asked him.

"Well you see, I've known Frangini for a very long time," Mr Cuewant said, "and while you were asleep, he came to me and told me all about you, he told me about dinner, your bed, the Tonkfar, everything, in fact we chatted for most of the night - that's why he was probably so tired this morning!"

The bell rang before Frank could ask Mr Cuewant about the Tonkfar and before he knew it, he was in Mr Anderson's classroom.

"Hello Frank, you're early today aren't you?" Mr Anderson said looking around at the deserted room.

After five minutes of waiting, Peter walked in.

"Oh, hi Frank," he said sitting down next to him. Peter whispered something but Frank couldn't hear it.

"What?" he asked.

"What was your dinner like, last night?" Peter repeated a bit louder.

Frank told Peter about dinner, the Tonkfar, sleeping in the foam bed, breakfast and the incident with Slake thinking he'd climbed over the security fence to get into the school, then being dragged down the corridor by him to Mr Cuewant's office.

After register Mr Anderson told the class to stay where they were and just talk quietly to each other. Ten minutes later, Mr Cuewant came into the class and said, "Can I have, *Frank Burray, Peter Puginic, Richard Gale, Melissa Goer* and *Annie Hawkes* in my office as soon as possible please?"

Frank and Peter stood up nervously, with the others, and then they all walked out of the classroom in single file. They trudged along at a slow pace until they got to Mr Cuewant's office. Frank pushed the door open to find Mr Cuewant standing there waiting expectantly for them, "Come on, come on, sit down." he said walking over to his desk.

"We're going to have a little spelling test to see who's going to compete in the Spelling Bee today. It's just a small test,

OK?" Mr Cuewant asked them.

They all got a piece of blank paper and Mr Cuewant read the words out. The words were quite easy so far, 'batteries', 'desperate', until the moment Frank dreaded happened. "Frequently," Mr Cuewant said.

'Frequently' was the hardest word to spell for Frank. He spelt it out in his head, 'F-R-E-Q-E-N-T-L-Y, no, F-R-E-Q-U-N-T-L-Y, no, F-R-E-Q-U-E-N-T-L-Y, yes' he thought to himself and he wrote it down. He knew he had to be in the top two of the group to qualify into the Spelling Bee and so far, he'd got most of them right. There were thirty spellings and by a quarter past nine, they'd got up to spelling twenty - five.

"Nearly finished! *Five more!*" Mr Cuewant said.

When they'd finished, Mr Cuewant said that they could go back to their class, and he would start marking their spellings. When Frank was walking back with Peter to Mr Anderson's class, he saw Mr Slake walking down the corridor straight at them. Frank tried to go to the right hand side of the corridor but unfortunately, when he walked past Slake, he was next to a dark room with the door open. Mr Slake quickly pulled him into the room and slammed the door. Frank was getting dragged again along a hard, cold floor with no carpet on it, and then he heard a door open and shut. A bright light was turned on and Mr Slake sat Frank down in a wooden chair. Mr Slake remained standing up and said in his usual quiet, and menacing voice, "Frank, you know that you climbed over the fence this morning, don't you?"

"WHAT? *NO!*" Frank said furiously.

A wide, evil grin slid onto Mr Slake's face. "You're spending your time in here, with me whilst I mark some exercise books."

"Well, what will I do?" Frank asked looking around the room.

"Lines!" he spat.

"WHAT! WHY?" Frank bellowed.

"BECAUSE YOU CLIMBED OVER THE FENCE!" Mr Slake shouted.

Frank looked up at him.

"Here," Mr Slake said handing him a sheet of lined paper.

"What shall I…?"

"I – Won't – Climb - Over - The – Fence – And- Then-Lie-About- It!" Mr Slake said quietly.

"How many times?" Frank sighed.

"Two - Hundred - Times," he said through his yellow teeth jabbing his greasy finger at Frank.

After nearly an hour of writing, Slake took Frank back through the dark room and into the corridor.

"Don't tell anybody about this Burray, or I will make you suffer." he whispered threateningly.

Frank looked up nervously at him. Mr Slake had a small smirk under his moustache, only so Frank could see.

"Now, get to class you little swine," Mr Slake said pushing him along the corridor.

He then disappeared back through the door.

When Frank had got back to Mr Anderson's classroom, Peter was curious about his disappearance.

"What happened? Was it Mr Slake?" he asked at break time.

"Look Peter, I'm not allowed to tell anyone," Frank said.

"Please!" Peter begged.

"OK, OK, fine. Come closer. Mr Slake caught me and made me write, 'I won't jump over the fence and lie about it', two hundred times! Four full pages!" Frank whispered even quieter than a mouse.

"WHAT?! HE CAN'T DO THAT!" Peter said.

Frank shivered. He felt cold breath on the back of his neck then a sinister voice spoke from behind Frank and Peter.

"And what may Mr Burray and Mr Puginic be doing here?" Mr Slake was standing right behind Frank (he spat when he said, 'Puginic' because he couldn't say it properly).

"Oh, hello, Mr Sla- What is that? Behind the wall!" Frank said widening his blue eyes and pointing at the wall on the other side of the playground.

When Mr Slake quickly turned around, he took enough time looking at the wall for Frank and Peter to go and hide behind a shed.

"BURRAY PUGINIC! I ORDER YOU TO SHOW YOURSELVES! YOU CAN'T HIDE FROM ME!" Mr Slake shouted furiously, looking around him.

Peter was trying really hard not to laugh. Finally, Mr Slake gave up looking for them and went back inside. Frank and Peter got out of their hiding place, and they ran straight back inside as they already were ten minutes late to lessons. After computing with Mr Worm, it was lunchtime but instead of going to the canteen, Frank, Peter and Lucy went to the Spelling Bee board outside Mr Slake's classroom as it was rumoured that the results were out. Nearly every corridor was empty when they walked down so it was easier to see who was on the Spelling Bee board. It read on the top of the piece of paper: ***SPELLING BEE CONTESTANTS!***

Frank glanced at the names on the sheet, *Timothy Francis, Harry Simpson, Rebecca Klope, Evie Dane, Fred Danish,* then the last five names on the sheet stood out from all the rest, *Jack Shaw, Sadio Lasogga, Lucy Dart, Peter Puginic and Frank Burray.* There were difficult spelling examples on a sheet of paper so they took a sheet each from the pile on the shelf under the notice board and stuffed it into their pockets.

"You do know that you have no chance of beating me or Sadio, right?" Frank turned around to see Jack and Sadio standing at the other end of the corridor smirking at them.

They started walking towards Frank, Peter and Lucy.

"Where's your idiot little friend, *Jackie*?" Peter said brushing his hair out of his face.

"Mind your own business, *fatso*," Jack laughed.

Then Mr Slake came running out of his classroom, "WHAT IS GOING ON HERE?!" He bellowed. He looked at Frank, Peter and Lucy. "There, there, play nicely you little swine. Burray and Puginic - I wasn't going to play at hide and seek at break time you know! And I'm still thinking of a suitable punishment for you both! NOW ALL OF YOU GET OUT OF MY SIGHT AND GO TO LUNCH!" He then stormed back into his classroom, slamming the door.

Not one of them hesitated, they all risked getting caught by another teacher for running as they ran down the corridor not looking back. When they got to the dinner hall, they got into the long line. After ten minutes of waiting, they finally got to the front and collected their lunches.

After school, Frank went straight home to practice his spellings. On his way there it was very windy and raining. He ran into the shed and went through his damp pockets to get out the sheet of difficult spelling examples, but he must've lost it because he found nothing except the Elf Chamber password and a few soggy tissues.

What did the password stand for? What did it mean? Frank decided rather than just sitting on his bed all night long, he'd try and workout what the password meant. *'Eht enots, eht enots, sah ot eb deyortsed ni eht rebmahc, ni eht dnomaid rafknot, Snilbog nos.'* What did it mean? Then Frank noticed something, in the last sentence, it said Snilbog! Frank read it over and over again until something came into his mind. 'Eht' said 'the' backwards. So what did it all say backwards? Frank was shocked when he found out what it meant. *'The stone, the stone, has to be destroyed in the chamber, in the diamond Tonkfar, Goblin son.'* He couldn't believe it, Snilbog meant Goblins. What did Natas mean then? *Satan Goblin!* Was Frank dreaming?

There was a sudden loud CRASH! just outside the shed, he leaped off the bed and peered through the window, feeling a bit nervous at what he might see. But he saw that it was just the fierce wind that had blown the big green bin over, crashing it first against the shed's wall making it rattle. Frank was tired, dry and warm now, so he didn't bother going out into the wind and rain to pick it up – it'd probably just blow over again anyway he thought! He decided to call it a day and got into bed and soon went to sleep.

Chapter 9- The Spelling Bee

The tumultuous beeping sound of the alarm woke Frank up on the day of the Spelling Bee. The last two days, (Wednesday and Thursday) had been pretty boring for Frank, Peter and Lucy. They'd heard nothing from Teethy, Frangini or the elves and Jack, Seb and Sadio had been constantly teasing them but always ran away when Lucy stepped forwards, but soon enough, it was the day of the Spelling Bee.

It was wet and cloudy outside and hardly anybody had woken up on Candlestick street. Frank got a banana he'd stolen from Grampa Joe the day before and had it for his breakfast. More people were getting up by the time Frank left to go to school and most were looking dull while they looked out of their windows. The cold waves were hammering against the sea wall and the football pitch was so muddy and churned up that there was hardly any grass on it at all.

When Frank got to school, expectations were running high. There were rumours and whispers when Frank walked past people as they must have found out that he was in the Spelling Bee. Shortly after sitting down in Mr Anderson's classroom, loud-mouth Jack was already telling Frank that he'd lose.

"Hey Bullsy, y'ready to lose?" Jack told him.

Frank just ignored him and kept concentrating on the whiteboard. He felt nervous because the whole year group would be watching him. When Peter walked in, Frank could tell he was feeling the exact same as he was. Peter just sat down and didn't speak. After register, Mr Anderson said, "Student's that are competing in the Spelling Bee, go down to the Hall, student's that aren't, go outside and head towards the hall at nine o'clock," and then he sat back down.

Frank, Peter, Lucy, Jack, Sadio and Tim stood up nervously, well not Jack and Sadio, and walked out of the door. Peter finally spoke, "Do you think the words will be really hard?"

"Not too hard." Frank assured him.

When Frank got into the hall, the contestants' brown benches were at the front of the hall. On the stage there was a small, golden cup. Everyone stared at the gleaming cup while taking a seat on a bench. Just then, Mr Cuewant walked quickly over towards the children.

"Hello children, sorry I'm a bit late. Now, don't get too worried, OK? The words aren't too hard, OK? Peter, are you OK? Right, if you're out, you go and sit with either the Lions, Snakes or Scorpions - whichever house that you're in. OK, are you all alright? No worries? Any questions?" Mr Cuewant said quickly.

Everyone kept silent and only glanced nervously at each other.

"OK, just stay here, I'll inform everyone in the playground that we're ready," Mr Cuewant said and he hurried back out of the door.

Peter sat there shaking, "Peter? Peter? Are you OK? Not too worried?" Frank asked.

He didn't answer. "Peter?" he repeated.

Peter turned his head and looked at Frank. They both sat there in silence for a moment, then Peter asked, "Are you nervous, Frank?"

"Yeh, I am. But it's only a few words that we have to spell in front of some people." Frank said, trying to make him calm.

"Yeh, s'suppose you're right," Peter said.

Just then, a man who was short, skinny and had a small black moustache with long, greasy black hair and a small, red hat on walked in. "Hello children," the man said shaking his hair out of his eyes. "I will be your judge today, if you don't know already, I'll say your name out and you'll come and stand in front of me," he said pointing towards a chair and table. "I'll say a word out, and you'll spell it. If you get it right, you'll sit back on the bench, get it wrong and you'll go sit down at your House table. The competition will keep going until there's a winner, who'll win that cup." Everyone looked up at the cup, the man was walking over to the door by the time they had looked back. "Oh, and I'm Mr Metal, Mr Moe Metal." and then he walked out.

"Who the hell was that?" Jack asked laughing.

"Well if you listened you might have actually found out

Jackie," Peter said.

"Don't cry, *Petey-weety,*" Jack smirked.

" - Says the guy who nearly cried when a pie went into his face!" Frank said.

Jack sat there silently after that and then Mr Anderson walked in with his class. After everyone had got in and all the other teachers with their classes were sat down, Mr Cuewant, who Frank hadn't realised had come back and sat down, stood up and said, "Hello children, I am happy to present the Spelling Bee today, now, be silent while Mr Metal explains what is going to happen."

Mr Metal stood up and told everyone what he'd told the contestants before everyone came in. Then the Spelling Bee began. Frank was sitting at the end of the bench.

"*Timothy Francis,* your word is *aggressive,*" Mr Metal said.

Timothy, with a brown shirt on, came up to the front of the hall. "Aggressive, a-g-g-r-e-s-s-i-v-e, aggressive," he said, Frank could see that his legs were shaking.

There was a slight pause and Mr Metal cheerfully said, "That is correct!" Timothy sat back down. "*Sadio Lasogga,* your word is *exaggerate,*" Mr Metal said.

Sadio stood up and walked over to the front of the hall, looking a bit more nervous that before.

"Exaggerate, e-x-a-g-e-r-"

"That is wrong! The spelling is e-x-a-g-g-e-r-a-t-e!" Mr Metal said widening his eyes. "Go sit down, Sadio!"

Sadio looked at Mr Metal and scowled. He walked slowly back to the Snakes' table and sat down with a dejected sigh.

"One down, nine to go! Now, *Jack Shaw,* your word is *yacht,*" Mr Metal said excitedly.

Jack stood up and looked around the hall breathing loudly. "Yacht, y-a-c-h-t, yacht," he said loudly.

"That is correct, Jack," Mr Metal said smiling. "*Harry Simpson,* your word is *concentrate,*"

Harry stood up brushing his long, black hair out of his face and walked to the front of the hall with his orange shirt on. "Concentrate, c-o-n-c-e-n-t-r-a-t-e, concentrate." he said.

"That is correct!" Mr Metal said cheerfully with a gleaming smile upon his face.

Harry sat back down. The next three children, (Rebecca, Evie and Fred), got their word right and then it was Lucy's turn, "*Lucy Dart,* your word is *tsunami,*" Mr Metal coughed.

Lucy stood up straight away, not trembling, shaking or breathing really loudly out of her mouth like Peter was, and walked normally towards the front of the hall. "Tsunami, t-s-u-n-a-m-i, tsunami," she said, not stopping or stammering at any point.

"That is correct!" Mr Metal cheered. "*Peter Puginic,* your word is equipment."

Peter, still trembling and shaking stood up and walked towards the marked out circle at the front of the hall. "E-equipment, e-q-u-i-p-m-e-n-t, equipment," Peter said.

Mr Metal sat there for a few moments, looking stunned and then said, "That is correct!"

That took away a bit of the apprehension from his face, then Frank's name was called out in a faint voice. Just then, Frank's knees started shaking and his legs were getting wobbly. He was getting dizzy for some reason and everyone was staring at him, which made him even more anxious. Then Peter nudged him and whispered, "Come on Frank, it's your turn!"

That made Frank even more apprehensive and he got up off the bench. He walked towards the front of the hall, now everyone was staring at him. Frank looked behind him and saw, Jack, Mr Slake, sitting next to Mr Cuewant, and Mrs Rose, who was sitting at the end of the table, smirking and watching Frank, probably thinking about what to say if he loses.

"Are you alright?" a voice said behind him. Mr Metal was sitting looking curiously at him and surveying Frank carefully.

"Yeh, I'm OK," Frank said, still dizzy.

"OK, spell *criticise,*" Mr Metal said.

Criticise was an easy word for Frank, he'd practised it all the time and he could spell it easily. Frank quickly said, "Criticise, c-r-i-t-i-c-i-s-e, criticise."

There was a slight pause, which felt like and hour to Frank, and then Mr Metal voiced echoed across the room, "That is correct, Frank!"

He let out a sigh of relief and sat back down, after Timothy, Jack, Harry and Rebecca, who all spelt their word right, except from Rebecca, who put two C's in necessary, it was back to Evie, "*Evie Dane,* your word is, *asylum.*"

Evie, who was next to to Harry now and had flaming, red hair, stood up and walked towards the front of the hall. All the boys in Snakes, along with Peter and Harry, were gazing at her not blinking or moving a muscle.

"What you looking at Peter?" Frank asked with a smirk on his face.

Peter did not answer. He just gazed at her, dreamily. Frank heard Lucy ask the same thing to Peter, again, he did not answer. Evie was in Snakes.

"Asylum, a-s-y-l-u-m, asylum," Evie said quickly.

"That is correct, Evie!" Mr Metal shouted.

A tsunami of applause erupted from the school, most of the

claps coming from the boys. Suddenly, Mr Cuewant stood up without warning, and the hall went silent. He surveyed the room, his eyes narrowed, and then he walked down the steps from the stage. He started running, left the Hall, and before Frank could blink, he was running down the corridor!

"OK children, let's get back to the Spell-" Mr Metal's speech was cut short by another person standing up: Sam Matthews. His face was paler than usual and his clothes were really messy, he also looked very poorly. He walked, very slowly out of the room and started to walk down the corridor. Everyone was shocked, you could tell as everyones' mouths were open.

"OK children, let's get back to the Spelling Bee, shall we?" he repeated. *"Fred Danish, your word is mountainside."*

Fred, a tall, black boy with brown hair and was in Mr Slake's maths group as well as Frank, stood up and walked, slowly and quietly towards the front of the room. "Mountainside, m-o-u-n-t-a-i-n-i-d-e, mountainside," Fred said confidently.

"That is wrong! The spelling is m-o-u-n-t-a-i-n-s-i-d-e, there are now only seven people left," Mr Metal said excitedly.

Fred went back to Scorpions table, looking gloomy and then it was Lucy's turn, *"Lucy Dart, your word is pacific,"* Mr Metal yawned.

"Pacific, p-a-c-i-f-i-c, pacific," Lucy said.

"That is correct!" Mr Metal cheered. *"Peter Puginic, your*

word is *ferocious.*"

Peter, who was a bit calmer and had had a confident smile on his face, went red and the smile was wiped off his face when he heard the word 'ferocious.' He stood up and walked towards the front of the hall, "Ferocious, f-e-r-o-c-i-o-s, ferocious," Peter said, not as confident as Lucy.

"That is wrong! The spelling is f-e-r-o-c-i-o-u-s," Mr Metal said.

Peter looked distraught, he walked over to the Lions table and then Frank's legs started trembling and he felt even dizzier as his name was called out. Then the worst possible thing happened, his word was: 'frequently'. There were faint footsteps running down the corridor when Frank got to the front, luckily, before Frank had to spell frequently, Mr Cuewant was at the door, his face all red and sweaty - he looked as if he'd just finished running in a marathon!

"Everybody outside, now," Mr Cuewant said normally. Nobody moved. "I SAID EVERYBODY OUTSIDE NOW! QUICKLY!" he bellowed, looking down the corridor.

Before Frank could even turn around to go to the fire exit, it was already packed with children and teachers pushing them along. Frank turned around, the other exit was also packed with children and teachers but not as many so Frank joined the crowd. Although Frank was in the middle of the pack, he could see what was slithering down the corridor. At least a twenty feet long great big fat python was slithering along the corridor, it's small, black and beady eyes looking around, its long forked tongue flicking in and out. It looked straight at Frank, who was now running through the crowd. Fresh air finally blew onto Frank's face when he got outside, there were children running everywhere, it was chaos. Frank saw Peter, Lucy and Harry running towards the football pitch so he ran towards them. Frank saw them run on a small playground, packed with lots of children already so he went with them. Unfortunately, Frank was at the front but he could hear Mr Cuewant talking to Mr Metal.

"What was it Maximus? A psycho? A giant spider? A- a, you know what?" Mr Metal asked trembling.

"What? NO! It was, it is Henry, it is a huge snake. His." Mr Cuewant whispered.

Mr Metal shuddered.

"What? How? Was it actually? His?" Mr Metal asked gripping Mr Cuewant.

"It's OK, Henry, we've checked the school, it's gone. We can't find it. It's gone, just disappeared!" said Mr Cuewant.

Frank stepped in between them, *"What? How come it's just gone? It was right there!"* He exclaimed.

"Frank, this is too complicated for you, you won't understand," Mr Cuewant said resting his hand on Frank's shoulder.

"How did the snake get in?" Frank asked.

Mr Cuewant glanced at Mr Metal, "I don't know," he said.

"No more questions, Frank," Mr Metal said.

"Will the Spelling Bee be carrying on again?" Frank asked curiously.

"No, probably not, not in the next few days anyway," Mr Metal said, his greasy hair blowing in his eyes.

"Who will get the cup?" Frank asked.

"Nobody will today, now go away and talk to your friends," Mr Metal said.

"But, who-"

"No more questions Frank, go!" Mr Metal said walking back towards the school.

"Great...I've now got to find Peter and Lucy in all this lot, what an onerous task," Frank muttered under his breath.

"FRANK!" Peter pounced onto Frank making him fall to the ground.

"Yeh, hi Peter, thanks for jumping on me," Frank said sarcastically.

"You're welcome! Anyway - what was it? I got outside before anyone else did - did you see it?" Peter asked.

Frank opened his mouth but Lucy came running up, "What was-"

"It was a bloomin' great big snake," Frank said.

"WHAT?" both Peter and Lucy said at the same time.

"How...? Did Mr Cuewant stop it?" Lucy asked.

"He did! He saved us! He told us all to get outside, and he went out earl-"

"Sam's a vampire!" Peter exclaimed, seeming to change the subject!

"Eh?! What? How...What you on about?" Lucy asked, still not believing that the rumour was true.

"Because, Snilbog's lives can sense when other lives are around. I think the snake is Snilbog's and Sam knew the snake was around, he knew everyone would be sent outside so he left earlier so he wouldn't be destroyed in the sunlight," Peter said looking up at the dark clouds. "So he went down the corridor so he didn't have to go outside because the teachers would force him out, that's evidence."

Lucy looked stunned, "Yeh, but-"

"What, so you think Sam just keeps making random noises for no reason, went normally out of the hall when a snake was nearby and avoided going outside?" Peter said, (Frank had noticed that he'd got a bit more lively after the snake was spotted).

"They can't find it, I heard Mr Cuewant talking to Mr Metal, Metal was like worried. He kept suggesting random things that it could have been, but Mr Cuewant told him, 'it was a snake, his...,' what does that mean?" Frank told them in a whisper.

"SEE!" Peter exclaimed. "The snake was Snilbog's! Even Mr Cuewant said it was!"

"Yeh, Peter, 'his' does not mean 'Snilbog's'!" Lucy said. "And what about the Spelling bee?"

"Mr Metal said it probably won't be held now, not for a few days anyway," Frank said.

DING DONG! DING DONG! A golden bell was been whacked with what looked like a golden hammer.

"EVERYBODY INTO THE HALL!" a teacher's voice shouted out but Frank couldn't see whose voice it was.

Frank, Peter and Lucy walked around the group of fourth years to the first years and got to the Hall much quicker than the rest of the children. The hall was packed with nervously excited children whispering to the person next to them. Frank saw a spot right at the back of the Hall so he headed down there, "What was it?", "I saw a killer clown with a knife!", "I ran literally so fast outside!", "I saw a giant monster with a snake!" Lots of rumours were getting exchanged in the hall.

Not many people were sitting near the back of the Hall

because they thought if the snake came back it would eat them first (that was also another rumour). After fifteen minutes of glancing down the vacant corridor and listening to Peter going on about Sam Matthews being a vampire, Mr Cuewant came running down the corridor, into the Hall and stood in the middle of the stage facing everyone.

"CHILDREN! BE SILENT! Now, some of you may have seen something unusual today - a big snake, but don't worry, you are all safe now, we've just checked out this part of the school, there's nothing there, it's gone. But from now on, always keep close to a teacher. The school inspector, the staff and lots of other people with be verifying that the school is totally safe. I don't know how long it will take to check the entire school so I will make sure someone, or something will tell you when school is back on," Mr Cuewant glanced towards where Frank was sitting when he said, 'something'.

"The school will not be running while we're searching it, I'll send an email letter out this morning to everyone so you won't forget, now everybody stay in here for another register, then you can all go home," and having said that he walked off the stage and out of the Hall.

An eruption of cheering and applause happened when Mr Cuewant was out of sight, Mr Slake and all the other teachers were trying to calm the school down but nothing stopped the cheers of happiness from all the pupils at this unexpected holiday! All except Frank however, who was not cheering, because he'd have to just go and sit in his shed. During the register Frank, Peter and Lucy just sat there talking quietly, and then, the register over, and everyone accounted for, it was home time.

"You may all leave, but go out of the school's main entrance – you *do not* climb over the walls or the fences – like some of you usually do!" Mr Slake shouted, picking out Frank and glaring at him!

Frank got up and walked out of the Hall to the main entrance, hanging back from the noise and crush of everyone else trying to get out all at the same time. He was soon alone and everything was quiet as he shuffled slowly out of the school door, with his bag on his back. He felt the cold breeze blow sharply into his face as he started to walk home alone.

Chapter 10- The Unexpected Arrival

Frank fell onto his bed. The next few days would be torture for him, unless he could find something really entertaining to do which would make the time go by quicker, but for now, he was lying on his bed looking up at the ceiling. He heard the back door to the house being opened and then slammed shut a few seconds later. A few seconds later the shed door opened quickly and a dark figure came in and stood just inside.

At first, Frank thought that it was a scary creature - but it was Grampa Joe who had walked in. (Frank was actually right, Grampa Joe looked like a scary creature with dark bags under his eyes wearing a dirty white shirt with some big baggy trousers on). Grampa Joe grunted and made loud footsteps with his big, black nob nailed boots as he walked towards Frank lying on his bed. Frank stared at him for a moment but before he could ask him anything, Grampa Joe said in a gruff voice,

"I just got an email, heard about the big snake attack, hoped it might've eaten you, but it obviously didn't...anyway...they're writing a report in the paper about your Headteacher, probably be sacked by the end of the term. He said that school will be starting on Monday morning as usual so you won't have to stay in this stinkin' shed all next week. Don't bother me or Molly though, we might feed you...maybe. So, yeh, see you next time I come in 'ere, and not before...y'understand?!" He didn't wait for Frank to reply, he just walked out of the shed, leaving a stinky smell behind.

What? What would he do if Mr Cuewant was sacked? Mr Slake would give him detention everyday! He lay there in silence for a few minutes, thinking what would happen if he was sacked. Who would be the Headmaster of Severors? Heavy rain from thick dark grey clouds suddenly started to pound on the roof and a strong wind was howling. Inside the shed it had gotten darker, and nothing could be heard except the rain and the wind. Candlestick Street had been deserted when Frank had walked down it a short while ago, he supposed everyone must've been expecting this storm.

After a while the wind slackened off and the rain drops on the roof were getting softer and quieter, *drop, drop, drop*, but just when he thought the storm might be over at last they started getting louder and louder - until something unexpected happened. *BANG! BANG! BANG!* It made Frank fall off his bed, the loud banging was coming from under his bed! He could feel the floor moving! He quickly got up and ran to the door, standing there almost paralysed in fear as he stared at the area his bed was on. He was ready to make a run for it outside despite the weather - but then a strong wind was blowing about inside the shed, knocking over several things.! It was like a mini tornado, he put his hands over his eyes, then it suddenly stopped - and another hand grabbed Frank's! He opened his eyes. Amazed, Frank felt his jaw drop. Mr

Cuewant was standing in the heart of the shed looking stunned!

"Ah! There you are! Hello Frank!" he said.

The wind had stopped but the banging was still going on,

"TEETHY! WILL YOU STOP IT!" Mr Cuewant shouted.

The banging stopped.

"Mr Cuewant, how did you-?" He stopped speaking as he heard the house's back door being opened again.

"You need to leave, now. It's my Grampa Joe!" Frank said.

"No problem, Teethy - keep quiet will you, a human is coming!" Mr Cuewant said and he disappeared in a yellow coloured whirlwind.

The moment the yellow wind disappeared, was the moment the door opened.

"ALRIGHT! WHO ELSE IS IN HERE? WOT'S GOIN' ON? I CAN HEAR YOU FROM INSIDE THE HOUSE YOU NITWIT! SHOW YOURSELF!" Grampa Joe bellowed while running into the shed.

"Grampa Joe, no - one's here! You must've just heard the storm!" Frank said trying to look confused and innocent at the same time..

"If you - let your friends - in'ere - you will not leave this shed - do y'unnerstand?" Grampa Joe whispered angrily.

135

"Yeh, yeh, yeh. OK!" Frank said.

Grampa Joe turned his back on Frank and opened the wooden door. He walked out and slammed it shut, he stood outside for a few seconds, looking around trying to get some evidence of anyone in the shed or nearby. But Mr Cuewant did not start to reappear until Grampa Joe had gone back inside the house. The mini tornado started again, and once again it knocked over a few things but after a few seconds of it spinning, it stopped. Mr Cuewant was standing in the middle of the room again, smiling at him!

"What are you doing here? And how did you do that?" Frank asked.

"I've come to take you to the Elf Chamber, of course!" Mr Cuewant said while he was lifting Frank's single bed up to reveal a square opening in the floorboards underneath it!

Teethy, Frangini, Peter and Lucy all pushed their heads through the gap.

"Peter! Lucy! - What are you all doing here?" Frank exclaimed but in a whisper.

"Is Mr Frank OK? Teethy heard about a big bad snake but Master's brother saves Mr Frank and Mr Peter and Miss Lucy!" Teethy squeaked.

"Yeh, I'm OK...wait...what?" Frank asked, confused.

"Yes, Frangini and I are brothers," Mr Cuewant said calmly.

"How? Are you actually an Elf - or something?!" Frank asked.

"No, he's not." Frangini said. "He's human, I used to be a human too but...well it's a long story... I'm now an Elf and here I am, an Elf, well, I'm half-Elf, half-human. My human name is Olivier Cuewant." Frangini said.

Frank was amazed. "How did you do that?" he asked Mr Cuewant.

"Olivier and I can do it, Elves have many unusual powers so if my brother is an Elf, I've got some powers as well," Mr Cuewant said.

"Can you - can you take people with you and can you go where you want?" Peter asked.

"Yes, yes I can, but we can only travel for a certain distance, say for example...if you wanted to go to Spain, well, we'd have to stop for a little rest every few hundred miles." Mr Cuewant said.

"Anyway - are you alright Mr Frank?" Frangini croaked.

"Yeh, I'm OK thanks! But Mr Cuewant - how come it said on the email you'll probably get sacked?!" Frank asked him, a lot of concern in his voice.

"I won't be! Don't worry! Next year I'll probably take some months off, I'll be back for your third year though, definitely," Mr Cuewant said.

"Who'll be the new Headmaster when you're away?" Lucy asked.

Mr Cuewant shrugged, "Haven't got a clue!" he said.

"Anyway, let's get back to the Elf Chamber before anyone finds out we're here!" Frangini said.

Mr Cuewant grabbed hold of Frank's arm and held it tight.

"Hold on, Frank," he said and then the wind started to blow again all around them.

Frank felt himself flying about for a few seconds and then it stopped. He had his eyes shut tightly so he couldn't see what had happened. Had they crashed or ended up in the wrong place? Frank opened his eyes; he was in a dark, narrow tunnel. He and Mr Cuewant could only just fit in it, they were stood still, side by side.

"Where are we?" Frank asked him, twisting his head to try and look around.

BANG! Another tornado of wind was spinning around behind Frank and Mr Cuewant. Then Lucy and Frangini reappeared, then Peter and Teethy.

Peter was looking around like he'd just woken up from a nap, and Lucy had a stunned look on her face.

"That was so weird!" Peter exclaimed.

"Come on then, let's go get ready for dinner, shall we?"

Frangini said.

After about half a minute the tube like tunnel widened out so they could all walk together in a line, but with Frangini leading the way. There were lots of turns and little passageways but they kept walking straight ahead. Finally, they got to the huge cave entrance, and looking in to it, just like last time, they saw it was packed with hundreds of Elves.

"Oh yeh, Frank, we're sleeping over as well, we told our parents we're sleeping over at a friend's house!" Peter said.

"Oh, wow!" Frank said.

"Is Mr Frank and Mr Peter and Miss Lucy OK?" Teethy kept repeating, fussing around them.

"Yes, Teethy, we're OK!" Frank said through his teeth.

"Teethy! Stop asking Mr Frank, Mr Peter and Miss Lucy if they're OK! - You can see they are!" Frangini said.

Then Frank noticed Teethy was wearing some ripped-up curtains for a jumper.

"Teethy, where's your jumper?" Frank asked looking around at the other Elves with brightly coloured jumpers on.

"Teethy lost it! Teethy has to wear this jumper now! Teethy likes this jumper but doesn't like it as much..."

"OK, then...would you like a new jumper for Christmas?" Frank asked.

"Oh yes, Mr Frank! Teethy loves jumpers! But isn't it only April?" Teethy squeaked.

"No, Teethy, it's *November!*" Frank laughed.

"Oh, Teethy did not know, I'm sorry Mr Frank."

"It's OK, Teethy, er, what's for dinner?" Frank asked him eagerly, as he suddenly felt really hungry.

"It's 'Italian Night' on Friday!" Teethy happily piped up.

Peter looked at him in surprise and said, "but...Teethy it's only *Wednesday* today!"

"Oh is it Mr Peter?! Well - never mind! *I was certain it was Friday...*" He said, scratching his head.

Frank didn't care what day it was because he loved Italian food: pizza, pasta, lasagne, ravioli and spaghetti, not that he had had any for a long time though…

"What shall we do until it's dinner time?" Peter asked looking at his watch. "It's only four o'clock."

"Teethy has to do something very important so Mr Frank and Mr Peter and Miss Lucy can go explore the Elf Chamber, goodbye!" Teethy said and he ran up the steps in The Elf Tower.

Then a small, familiar Elf with a bright green jumper on, came running up to Frank.

"Mr Human! Mr Human! Parry can talk to you finally! Parry has always wanted to talk to Mr Human! What is Mr Human's name?" The Elf cheeped shaking Frank's hand.

"I'm Frank, this is Lucy and this is Peter, Parry," Frank said.

"Mr Frank and other humans! Parry welcomes you!" The Elf squeaked. "I'm Parry!"

"Oh, Hi Parry!" Lucy said.

"Oh, hello Mr Peter," Parry squealed with delight as he shook Lucy's hand. He then started shaking Peter's had and said,

 "Hello Miss Lucy! Parry has to go now! Goodbye!"

He then ran across the cave towards a small door.

"What shall we do now?" Peter asked shaking his head in amusement at Parry's mixing up of their names.

****

It was five minutes before dinner time when the elves started to make the foam table. Mr Cuewant had left at six o'clock and Frangini and Teethy were still nowhere to be found.

"They could be upstairs," Frank suggested.

"Yeh, they will be," Lucy assured them.

At five minutes past seven, Frangini and Teethy both came running down the steps of The Elf Tower.

"Are we late? Just having a nap, I was up all night last

night!" Frangini laughed. "Time for dinner!"

All the Elves, just like last time Frank was there, ran down to the kitchen to get the food.

"Wow!" Peter said, flabbergasted.

"Foam tables! Wow, that's amazing!" Lucy exclaimed.

Then, a few seconds later, the Elves emerged from the passageway carrying large plates and bowls filled with all sorts of Italian food. Pasta, pizza, spaghetti, ravioli - everything you'd expect to get to eat in Italy! A giant Italian flag of red, green and white floated down from the ceiling of the cave, and it flapped about as if a strong wind was blowing it, above the long table as all the food was being put on it.

"SIT!" Frangini roared.

There was a big red chair for Frank and green and yellow ones for Peter and Lucy. Frangini had plonked himself into an orange one at the far end of the table. He was resting both of his hands on the arms of the chair then he lifted himself up from it, took a deep breath and shouted, "HELLO ELVES! THANK YOU FOR THIS ITALIAN DINNER TONIGHT! SO - LET THE FEAST...BEGIN!"

Frank's plate was full of ravioli and he started on it seconds after the word 'begin' was shouted. The food smelt and looked delicious. It took him nearly half an hour to eat his main course, as he helped himself to a third helping! He knew that lots of pudding would soon be coming up from the kitchen as well!

Their plates and bowls empty, Frangini was sat, like Peter and Lucy, on his chair, holding his stomach.

"I - I can't fit any- anymore in!" Peter gasped.

"Unlucky for you then! – I've saved some room! 'Cause there's loads of pudding still to come," Frank laughed.

"What?" Peter moaned, he then made a loud groan and shut his eyes.

"Are you tired, Peter?" Frank asked.

He didn't answer.

"He's fallen to sleep," Frangini said. "Mr Frank, will you shout the Elves to come and take him? I can't. I'm too full!"

"Where...where shall I tell them to take him?" Frank asked.

"Don't worry they'll know! Just shout!"

"ELVES! COME AND TAKE HUMAN!" Frank bellowed down the table.

A dozen Elves got up and ran to where Peter was slumped back in his chair fast asleep, and carefully lifted him up. They ran over to a corner of the cave and put him back down onto some foam like a mattress on the floor. They then left him and ran back to the dinner table. Peter's head fell sideways and then he slowly fell onto his back.

"D'you think he's OK?" Lucy asked, looking over to Peter who was now snoring loudly!

"He'll be fine, I think it's time for pudding," Frangini yawned.

Frank, instead of having loads of pudding like last time, just had two medium sized sweet fruity tarts covered in thick cream, as he was actually more full from the three helpings of ravioli than he'd thought! Between mouthfuls he talked to Lucy about the Tonkfar.

"Maybe Peter was right, maybe Sam is the stone...so have you worked out the message?" Lucy asked looking at Frank.

"Yeh, it means that the stone has to be destroyed *in the Tonkfar*, Lucy," Frank said.

Unfortunately, Frangini overheard them speaking about the Tonkfar, "Been a bit mischievous, eh? Look, I must warn you - the Tonkfar has got a very dark meaning to it," his voice suddenly dropped and a cold breath came out of his mouth. "Something very, very dark."

Lucy looked nervous at hearing this

Frangini's voice came back to normal, and he said, "Well, anyway...I'll talk about it another time! - It's now Time For Bed!"

Once again, the Elves got busy making three mini houses out

of foam for their guests to sleep in, all placed neatly in line next to each other. Lucy was too busy to even look at the houses as she was talking to Apple. When the making of the houses had finished, she looked up and was astonished.

"How? They – did – what? – how?! How did they make those so quickly?!" She stammered. "Are we, are we sleeping in them? They look so comfy!"

"Yeh, it's like really comfy, I didn't wake up once last time I slept in one!" Frank said.

"Can't wait! I'm feeling dead tired now as well!" Lucy said with a big yawn.

Again, a dozen Elves ran over to Peter and lifted him up carrying him towards the house on the left, they went inside and dropped him onto the soft foam bed. The elves then ran out and came back with either covers or pillows in their hands. They chucked the covers onto the snoring Peter and threw the pillows onto his head. The Elves then made up Frank's and Lucy's beds with clean sheets and pillows. While they were neatly making them up , Lucy noticed the Tonkfar which had been left open once again.

"Is that the Tonkfar?" she whispered pointing towards it.

"Yeh," Frank said.

"So it's that what Peter says you have to put Sam in?! If it is there's no way he'll fit in there!" She exclaimed in a whisper.

"I know that! I'm not that thick!" Frank muttered.

"TIME FOR BED!" Frangini roared, having obviously got his voice back!

Frank sauntered into the middle house and sat on his bed, quietly.

"Alright, lights out in one minute!" Frangini bellowed.

"Goodnight!"

As soon as they were tucked up in their beds the lights went out, but Frank lay wide awake in his bed for a long time pondering how would they fit Sam Matthews into the Tonkfar? Let alone get him anywhere near it! Then he thought no more and fell asleep.

****

Frank woke up to a humming sound at five o'clock. Peter was sitting o the floor at the foot of Frank's bed, he was humming loudly!

"Peter, what the hell are you doing?" Frank yawned while rubbing his eyes.

"I woke up on the floor over in the corner buried under all my covers and pillows! It was at about half an hour ago. I've been sitting here humming since then!" Peter whispered.

"Er, Peter, why? Why've you just been sitting there - humming? Oh I'm still tired!" Frank said closing his eyes.

"Wake up! I want you to talk to me, I'm bored!" Peter hissed. "I've also been staring at the Tonkfar, humming helps me to concentrate, I'm thinking about-" he yawned, fell backwards onto the floor and started snoring again!

Frank sighed, shrugged, turned over and after a minute was nearly asleep again - but he was fully awoken by footsteps in the cave.

"Peter?" he asked turning over.

Frank opened his eyes wider and sat up when he saw that Peter was still asleep on the floor. So who was it creeping around?

"Is anybody there?" Frank called out.

Silence.

"Hello! Who's there?" A bit louder this time.

Then he heard the footsteps running across the cave away from him towards the far corner. Sitting up in bed he saw the dark outline of a figure running towards the Tonkfar!

Frank got out of bed and ran for the culprit who was now over half way across the cave.

"Lucy? Frangini? Teethy?" Frank called out trying to get a better look at who it was.

He was bewildered when he saw a familiar face now standing in front of the Tonkfar - a very pale and sinister looking face that had slowly turned to look at him.

"Sam...is it you?!" Frank exclaimed but not quite sure.

Sam hissed loudly like a snake and turning away from Frank he grabbed at the door of the Tonkfar. He started pulling at it quickly, almost in a panic. Frank had no idea why Sam was doing that until he too heard lots more footsteps running down the steps leading up to the Elves' rooms.

"What is all this racket?! Who's there?" Frangini shouted, he was accompanied by Teethy, Parry, Apple and half a dozen other small, long nosed Elves all carrying small lanterns.

"What is that, Master?" Teethy was petrified.

"It's Him! The Thief of Snilbog!" Frangini shouted. "Mr Frank, put Mr Peter back in his house and into bed, and get back into bed yourself and stay there where you'll be safe!"

Frank didn't hesitate. He ran back into his foam house for Peter, put his arm around his shoulders, struggling a bit because of his weight. All the shouting had now woken Lucy up as well. She came running out of her little house and ran to Frank and Peter.

"NO!" Frangini bellowed, looking at Lucy. He held his right hand above his head and pushed it forwards.

A flash of red light appeared which made Lucy and Peter suddenly hover above the floor.

"Recni!" The old Elf bellowed.

Peter went flying into his house, falling onto his bed with such force it made the foam house collapse! Then Lucy started to move and once again, Frangini shouted, "Recni!"

She also went flying backwards and smashed into the foam wall, also making her house collapse. Frank's house, which was in the middle was demolished as Lucy's and Peter's had toppled onto it.

"Frank, get under the blocks of foam!" Frangini yelled, great concern on his face.

Frank leapt for the blocks and crawled under them; he couldn't see what was happening, he only heard the yells from Frangini. He moved forwards to get a clear view. Sam, now cornered by the Elves, had an evil grin on his face, he clapped his hands three times and disappeared in a puff of smoke!

Chapter 11- The Dragon Cave

The Elves fell to the ground.

"I'd better inform The Ministry straight away." Frangini said letting out a big sigh.

"What's *'The Ministry'*?" Frank asked him, getting up from under the foam blocks, and now very much wide awake.

"The Ministry of Elves, it's where King Elf lives, and where all the smart Elves work," Frangini answered.

"But you're smart, Frangini. How come you don't work there?" Frank said.

"It's for the really smart Elves Frank. I actually used to work there but I decided to retire a few hundred years ago!"

"What did you do, like what job?" Frank asked him.

"I was an Elf Judge and sentenced bad Elves to the Elf prison, *Winsinskop.*" Frangini said dreamily.

"Wow! *An Elf Judge*?" Frank asked.

"Yes, indeed I was, I'll have to go to The Ministry now, I'll see you nearer to Christ-" Frangini was surprised when Frank interrupted him.

"Can I come?" Frank asked.

"You? Er...wait...er...are you willing to do this?" Frangini whispered.

"Yes! Can Peter and Lucy come as well?" Frank asked looking around for them.

"Yes, OK, be sensible though, and you'll have to do what I tell you when we get there - OK? We'll be travelling the same way we got here with Maximus yesterday," Frangini said.

Frank turned around. He could hear Peter's snoring, he was hidden under the blocks of foam, obviously still in a deep sleep. Lucy, however, was wide awake and like Frank she was looking perplexed. She was standing next to Apple, having just climbed out from under the protective foam blocks.

"How did Sam do that? And how did he get here anyway?" She called out running towards Frank.

"I don't kno! Frangini said that we can go with him to the Ministry of Elves! It's where King Elf lives and a lot of smart Elves work and stuff like that, Frangini used to work there as like a Elf Judge sentencing bad Elves to the Elf prison, it's called something like Winkytall." Frank said.

"Oh, is Peter allowed to come too?" Lucy asked looking over at the blocks of foam which had a snoring boy under them, who, between snores was talking about bacon and banana sandwiches in his sleep!

"If he wakes up, yeh!" Frank joked.

"Are you ready? We'd better be off, mustn't delay!" Frangini said quickly to Frank and Lucy.

"Wait - what about Peter?" Lucy asked the old Elf.

"Don't you worry, now get hold of an arm each, and hold tight, keep your eyes closed when we go, Peter will be coming with us as well!"

Frank grabbed Frangini's right arm, and Lucy his left. Peter felt himself getting pulled around and his hair flapping about in a sudden ferocious wind. He opened his eyes a fraction to see a bright, yellow light but instead of Frangini to his left, he saw nothing but lots of empty space. Where were they? Was he supposed to keep his eyes shut all the time? Had he been flying into a different galaxy? The light dimmed and Frank was hovering horizontally inches above the ground, on his stomach. *Thump!* Frank had fallen flat on the floor. A firm hand gripped his and lifted him up onto his feet.

"Do not open your eyes, Frank!" Frangini shouted.

"We've been waiting for ages..." Lucy said now on her feet having been lifted up as well.

The roar of a snore interrupted her. Peter was still asleep on the floor and snoring really loudly now, but something even louder took over the snoring sounds in the tunnel. An ear – piercing roar knocked Frank over back onto the floor.

"Are we here, I mean, are we *there* yet?" Frank asked getting back to his feet.

"No, we're not, we'd better get to our next stop straight away it sounds like something's coming something we might not want to meet!- Hold on to my arms again." Frangini said slightly out of breath.

Lucy grabbed on to his arm but before Frank could, they had all disappeared, along with Peter. Frank was now alone in a dark tunnel which was in a dim mysterious place. What should he do? Frangini would surely show up for him, wouldn't he? Frank didn't know if he should stay where he was or go and explore. He decided to explore the place and see what was there. He walked along the long tunnel which seemed like it never ended; there were passages going left, some going right and some even moving up and down the walls.. Finally, after what felt like hours of walking, he came across a large, dimly lit chamber.

Entering it Frank sank upto his knees in tiny grains of sand that were brown and quite warm. There was a large bump in the middle of the room but everywhere else was flat. Frank was standing in the only exit there was; all of the walls were covered in dirt, hard mud and sand. He took one large step forward through the sand and paused listening for any movement, but all was dim and quiet. Frank silently stepped towards the bump but went around it first, just to make sure that nothing hideous was sleeping there, Frank hoped it was just a lot of sand in one place so he moved on; little did he know though, that he was wrong…very wrong...

Behind the lump of sand, he saw that there was a very large

old chest which looked like something you'd see full of treasure in a Pirate film. It opened with a creak when Frank touched the two locks on it. Amazed, he looked saw a gleaming, white metal sword with *His, written* on it's handle. Frank reached out to hold it and he was so concentrated on the sword, he didn't realise there was movement behind him.

"Who Goes There?" A voice hissed.

Frank turned around to find a giant, hideous creature; a red bodied, green - eyed dragon with massive wings half raised up!

He shouted, "HELP! SOMEBODY! HELP!"

"There's no point shouting you stupid human boy! They can't hear you, no one can – only me!" The dragon cackled as it said this. Frank looked around the chamber desperate to find somewhere to hide or escape, as he glanced towards a corner his heart sank when he saw a large pile of charred bones part covered in the remains of burnt ripped up clothes...

"D,D,Did Y,You-" He gasped pointing at the pile...

"Yes I Did! I barbecued them and ate them for finding out about that!" The dragon hissed looking at the sword. "So now, I, the dragon Tambos, say that you have to die too!" And he opened his mouth wide.

A breath of fire spewed out of his mouth, luckily missing Frank by an inch as he leapt to one side frantically.

"You can't escape Tambos human boy! I shall crush your

bones you..." and Tambos the dragon let out another roar of fire.

Frank knew he couldn't stay there so he made a run for it. Another tsunami of fire came out of his mouth and again, just missed Frank. **BANG!** Instead of wind, Frank was saved by a puff of bright smoke. Frangini, Mr Cuewant, Lucy and Peter who was now awake were standing in a huddle behind Tambos.

"FRANK! RUN TO US!" Mr Cuewant bellowed.

He didn't hesitate, he ran as fast as he could towards the petrified Peter and Lucy. The dragon let out a thunderous roar and a wave of fire, nearly hitting Peter this time, but it scorched his trousers.

Frank leaped towards Mr Cuewant but Tambos made sure he got nowhere near him. He whipped his long, red tail and hit Mr Cuewant, Frangini, Peter and Lucy sending them all flying to the other end of the room, crashing into the wall.

"What a feast I shall have tonight!" Tambos got ready to breathe out more fire which he was aiming straight at Frank this time. Mr Cuewant together with Frangini pushed their hands towards Frank and they sent a barrier force field to surround Frank making him invisible as well. The stream of fire bounced off the barrier around Frank, letting him make a run for it. He hid behind the large trunk which had the sword in it.

"You can't hide! Come out, come out!" Tambos bellowed

letting out more spraying fire, which went nowhere near Frank.

"FRANK, RUN LEFT!" Frangini shouted.

He got out of his hiding place and ran left; luckily the dragon was facing right. On the other hand, the unlucky thing that happened was that he stumbled over a large rock buried in the knee deep sand whilst he was running which caused him to fall over.

"I warned you, I told you - you can't escape from *ME!*" The dragon cackled again while edging forwards towards the area of disturbed sand where Frank was. Even though the dragon couldn't see him it was obvious where he was...

"*NO!*" Mr Cuewant shouted and then muttered something quickly.

"YOU!" The dragon roared! "Mr Maximus Cuewant! Aren't you the Headteacher of a school of baboons, and...one of *His*?"

"YES! IT IS I! And what's that I see, a sword that's *His?*" Mr Cuewant then actually chuckled, "YOU! Tambos The Dragon! It has come to my attention that you are guarding something, and I think I know exactly what it is! I know because I've been sent a mission, and I have to complete it." Tambos started to let out a roar and a breath of fire, but this time something very unexpected happened.

Instead of just fire, a blazing skull like face appeared and let

156

out a massive howl as it glided towards Mr Cuewant.

Surprisingly Mr Cuewant waited until the skull was right in front of him, only then did he hold up his hand and bellow, "SALANDIO!"

The face backed away and flew back into the dragon's mouth.

"WHAT?! - NOBODY HAS EVER SURVIVED THE FACE! FOR THAT I TAMBOS SHALL KILL YOU NOWWWWW!" The dragon roared and spewed out another tsunami of fire.

Mr Cuewant had grabbed Frank and they disappeared from the scene. Soon after their departure, Frank could feel the cold air of the wind hit his face, the tornado was pushing him away then it stopped suddenly, they were back in the Elf Chamber.

"Mr Frank! Mr Frank!" Teethy cried. It seemed Frangini, Peter and Lucy had beaten them back but they were all on the floor, "Teethy just heard what happened with the, d-d-dragon! Is Mr Frank OK?"

"Yes Teethy, I'm OK! I think!" Frank could barely mutter, so great was his relief at being rescued.

"Frank, Peter, Lucy, meet me in Frangini's room in five minutes, please," said Mr Cuewant said in a rush - and he disappeared again.

"He sounded worried, we'd better go up," Lucy whispered.

Peter glanced towards Frank and started to try and catch up to

Lucy who was already at the stairs. Frank couldn't believe what he had just gone through, having been alone and then escaped a dragon, he felt really grateful to Mr Cuewant as he had just saved him from being barbecued! He started to run as he was getting left behind the duo who by now were well in front of him. On the way up the stairs, Frank did not see any Elves walking up or down. It was only about seven o'clock and it had felt like a whole day already, what with Sam Matthews breaking in and disappearing before his eyes, wandering alone for ages in that tunnel and then fighting a dragon and escaping death!

"Come on in everyone, sit down!" Mr Cuewant said when they opened the creaky door. "Now, Frank, we could have got to you earlier this morning but there was something stopping us, and that's why I want to talk to you all. So...Frank, I need to know what the dragon Tambos said and did exactly? Sorry if I'm asking you to relive that unpleasant experience but it is really important I know!"

"Well, er...I went to explore and found that big chamber with the sand in. There was a lump in the sand and a chest behind it, with a sword in it which had 'His' written on it. I think I picked it up and then Tambos appeared and said that I have to die because I'd found out about it.

He pointed towards some bones and said they were people he'd eaten because they'd found the sword and then he breathed out fire at me! He kept, kept trying to burn me! And I was running - and then you lot saved me!" Frank explained, breathing deeply as he played the terrifying events back in his mind.

"Yes, yes, yes, thank you Frank...well, it's quite obvious that some...something, some force, wanted you to die, and that force was stopping us – getting to you straight away - but together me and Frangini were stronger and got past it, then we found you, with Tambos. Now...I think I know what it was stopping us," Mr Cuewant whispered.

"What? What was it?" Frank, Peter and Lucy all asked at the same time.

There was a pause, "I may be wrong but I think it was, the... *Goblins,*" Mr Cuewant said. "Something wanted you dead, hoping that the dragon would kill you before we got there, because *it* knew we'd win and save you. But now, the sword is in danger! But Frangini and I are powerful and we'll get it, we know where it is now, and we know how to get it!"

"Well...why? Why do you need it?" Peter asked.

Suddenly, something came to Frank's mind, "It's one of his lives, isn't it?" he exclaimed.

"What are you talking about?" Mr Cuewant laughed nervously.

"You know what I'm talking about! Snilbog's lives!" Frank said.

"OK, OK! It is one of his lives! Now, anyway, you cannot go to the Ministry of Elves, not today, not after the shock of these events you have gone through. Frangini has already gone and you'll have to go home, have the chance to rest and recover from them. I'm sorry you couldn't go but, I'm sure you'll be able to go next time, soon.. Come on then, let's go down!"

They all stood up and went back down together to the main part of the Elf Chamber, Frank was still trembling slightly...

Chapter 12- Sacked

The rest of the day had been cold and grey and Frank had been alone in the shed, but it hadn't been as boring as it usually was. The Elves had given Frank lots of food in sacks which he'd hidden under his bed, and he had just been watching football on a small portable television they'd brought for him as well. So he'd spent the day watching different matches and eating his food whilst thinking about everything that had happened that morning. He couldn't believe it! *I fought a dragon today!* He kept saying to himself. Frank had never thought that dragons were actually real - until that morning!

Night came and there were bright stars and a big full moon in the cloudless sky. There was still plenty of food left: cooked sausages, cornflakes, chocolate, oranges, various cheeses and a packet of crackers, and a few more bits of food. It was eleven o'clock when Frank ate his last bar of chocolate and fell back onto his bed. He wondered what would happen next year; *'I'll probably take some months off.'* Those were the words Mr Cuewant had said to him, and they had been lingering in his mind. Frank was really tired and nervous about what would happen the next day. Maybe he'll be attacked by a giant banana, a talking book or a crazy psycho like Grampa Joe; anything was possible! He'd thought Elves and dragons weren't real until he was actually face to face with them so what else was? He turned the light off, then back on again as he thought he'd better hide the little portable television under the bed. That done he turned the light off again, closed his eyes, and soon fell into a deep sleep in the silent, cold shed.

It was still dark when Frank woke up at six o'clock the following morning, even though he'd turned his alarm off last night, and he reached out and switched the light on.

He got out of bed, put his slippers on and looked through the tiny gap where he could see Erny's television. His front room was dark and quiet so that meant he was still in bed.

The cold November wind was howling at Frank's window, and rain was thrashing on the small shed window. He shuddered in the cold air and got back into bed to read a few more chapters of his book: 'Harry Potter and the Order of the Phoenix'. Frank liked reading books, mainly long books. At ten o'clock it was a bit lighter outside but still wet and grey. Grampa Joe came into the shed, "Here, made breakfast, made bacon and eggs, and there was still an egg so here!"

Frank took the plate with what looked like a mouldy, half cooked egg with a few drops of old brown sauce on it, waited for Grampa Joe to leave and shut the door, and dashed out to chuck it over the fence into the new neighbours - Mr and Mrs Jacksons' - garden. He hadn't spoken to the new neighbours since they had moved in, he'd observed that they were normally outside gardening or inside watching television.. Mr Jackson was a very thin man who wore round glasses, he had a small curly moustache, a pale bald head and always wore a black suit.

Mrs Jackson, however, was a very fat lady with a large slack mouth, long tatty grey hair and looked like an evil witch as she always wore a purple cloak. Their house lights were on and Frank looked up to see Mrs Jackson who was at the back bedroom window, looking down at Frank with an unpleasant expression on her face. She then turned around and walked out of his sight back into the room.

BANG! There was a flash of red smoke and then at the foot of Frank's bed, a newspaper sat there.

Frank quickly went back into the shed, he snatched up the paper, expecting to find a bloody hand or something else just as hideous under it, but nothing lay under it. Would anything happen if he opened the paper? Frank cautiously opened the mysterious newspaper which was called 'The Severor Sun'. The first thing he saw caught his eye, was the big headline, it was titled:

Severors Suffers Sneaky Slithering Snake Attack!

Frank read on,

Severors Secondary School has been attacked by a snake! Fortunately, nobody got hurt or injured but this is quite serious. The first-years were in the middle of a Spelling Bee when the snake tried to attack them. Maximus Cuewant, Headmaster of Severors, has released a statement that the school is safe and it will be open again on Monday 16th

November. Maximus claims that he apparently, 'saved' the children by sending them outside and handling the monster sized python himself! He is an irresponsible madman and will not be participating as Headmaster next year, we have interviewed him and he has told us, "The snake disappeared before my eyes when I chased it, it slithered down the corridor, while I was running after it. It disappeared and I went back outside!"

All the teachers think he is crazy. Luke Slake, a well liked and very popular maths teacher at Severors, has told us, "None of the teachers like him, I am, and all the other teachers are as well - quite relieved that he'll be leaving next year! He's stupid! A boy named Frank Burray keeps climbing over the fence which is against the rules, and Maximus still keeps letting him off! School discipline is going to pot! This is no way to run our great school! He's an idiot!"

Emma Buckle has also interviewed Rebecca Rose, an art teacher who works at Severors, and she has told us more about Frank Burray. "He's Cuewant's favourite! He and his two other friends knocked out three nice helpless children that they bully, but guess what? Maximus still let him off and now the three boys are getting badly bullied every day by them! Frank Burray is a wild little brat and he always argues with and is very rude to every teacher he comes across!"

The school are still trying to find a new Headmaster for next year so your children will be safer from the likes of Burray and his violent gang. I hope you feel a bit calmer after reading this, if Maximus Cuewant harms your child, tell the police and contact us at 66729399112.

Frank was burning with anger after reading this nonsense! Why had they only interviewed the two teachers that hated him? Why had the newspaper reporter believed them? Now everyone will think that he was a massive troublemaker! And Mr Slake had told The Severor Sun that Frank had climbed over the fence, that no teachers liked Mr Cuewant and he'd be happy when he leaves! He hoped Mr Cuewant would sack him before he leaves or Mr Slake would make him spend two-thirds of his year in detention! Frank reread the false news article several times until lunchtime and then he finally had to put the paper down before he boiled over in anger and frustration! How dare he! Mrs Rose had acted stupid as well, *'Three helpless children that they bully! The three boys get badly bullied!'* Stupid lying woman! Jack and his 'helpless' friends don't get bullied! They're the bullies! But sometimes they just pick on the wrong people and they get a taste of their own medicine – which served them right! Frank spent the rest of the day on his bed reading his book. There was still enough food for several days left in the sacks under the bed, so he didn't need to risk going into the house to scavenge any from in there.

The days passed by and on Sunday evening he decided that because it was Monday the following day, and the school was open again after the snake's attack, he'd get a good night's sleep so he turned over and because he'd been up early that morning, it wasn't hard to fall asleep.

BEEP! BEEP! BEEP! BEEP!

"OK, OK! I'm getting up!" Frank yawned widely.

BEEP! BEEP! BANG! Frank whacked the top of the alarm and it shut up. Frank for once didn't feel tired at all that morning; in fact he felt the liveliest he had been all year. By the time he had got dressed and ate an apple pie from the Elves, more and more lights were going on in all the neighbours' houses, so people were getting up which meant it was time for them to get ready go to work, and for him to go to school. He checked his alarm clock which proved him right; it was a quarter to eight. The shed door made a loud bang when it closed and the side gate which lead out into the street also made a loud bang. *The first thing I'll do is go to Mr Cuewant's office and ask him if he's sacked Slake yet! W*as the main thing going through his mind. When Frank got to school, he felt really uncomfortable around the other children. There were whispers like, "Isn't he Frank Burray The Bully?". "He was in the paper!" and "Apparently he's Mr Cuewant's favourite student!"

Frank, however just walked past them and into the main area of the school. *Knock, knock.*

"Come in," a voice said.

Frank pushed the door open and found Mr Cuewant sitting normally in his squishy armchair, his hands folded on top of the wooden desk.

"Sit down, Frank," Mr Cuewant said calmly.

Frank sat down and waited for Mr Cuewant to say something.

"What would you like to say, Frank?"

"Well...er...have you seen The Severor Sun?" Frank asked him.

"Yes."

"Er...aren't you gonna sack Mr Slake and Mrs Rose?"

"Yes, I will, be aware though, this may be the last time you have a maths lesson with Mr Slake, and maybe your last art lesson with Mrs Rose, it will depend..."

"Oh, OK...well...bye then!" And then Frank turned around and went outside. That was quick, he told himself. "OK, what've I got today?"

Frank pulled out the crinkled piece of paper which was his timetable and read it in a whisper.

" First lesson, maths with Slake, next art with Rose, PE with Johnson, RE with Abs and Science with Solte."

He let out a groan.

"Maths, Art and PE, and that's only in the morning, awful,

but RE and Science aren't too bad even though they're both really boring. I wonder what Peter's got today?"

Everyone was inside by now because the corridors were filled with kids and when Frank walked into Mr Anderson's class, nearly every seat was occupied. The room went silent as he sat down next to Peter. "Psst, Peter."

"What?"

"I've just been to see Mr Cuewant and he said it might be the last time Slake teaches us! Do you know what this means?" Frank said excitedly.

"Er..."

"It means he'll be sacked!" Frank whispered.

"Oh, nice one! What about Miss Rose?" Peter asked.

"He said 'maybe' she will as well!" Frank told Peter.

"Oh, just ignore these kids that are looking at you, they're jealous that there not in the paper!"

"I'm actually looking forwards to ma-"

"*Frank Burray.*"

"Here!"

The corridors were packed with children on the way down to maths. Frank kept an eye out for Sam Matthews because of what happened last week; but he was nowhere to be seen.

Frank waited outside with Peter for Mr Slake to open the door while everyone stared at them. The door opened and Mr Slake stepped out.

"IN!." Mr Slake said through his yellow teeth in a sinister voice.

Nobody dared to move.

"IN, I SAID!" he then bellowed at them.

Finally, Johnny Devas moved into the classroom and so did the other children. Frank looked up at Slake when he walked past him; he had a smirk on his face but Frank imagined what his ugly face would look like when he found out the he was sacked. Mr Slake also gave Frank a shoulder barge as he walked in the same time as him. The maths room was dark and all the curtains were shut. Frank walked to the back until he heard a voice say his name.

"Where do you think you're going, Burray? You're sitting at the front!" Slake snarled.

Frank let out a sigh and sat at the desk which the teacher was standing next to.

"You've got a great lesson coming up, Frank," Slake whispered, his voice then went louder so the whole class could hear him. "Now, you may have heard that this little pig has been in the paper, and climbed over the fence."

"I DID NOT CLIMB OVER THE FENCE!"

"Detention, after school for arguing!" Mr Slake snapped. "So, today, instead of doing some maths - you're going to tell your fellow students how much you like being laughed at and how your magnificent escape from a lifetime of detention went . But, when your beloved Headmaster is sacked, believe me, you'll get detention everyday. Now, get up pig and stand at the front of the class, then tell them what happened. No – one's leaving until you explain."

Frank stood up, trying not to shout out it's Slake's last lesson, and walked to the front of the classroom. "I don't like been laughed at and I didn't clim-"

"YES YOU DID!" Slake shouted.

Frank then just stood there not saying anything for five minutes. The whole class was silent just like Frank.

"I told you, nobody leaves until you tell what-"

There were three knocks on the door. "What?" Slake grunted.

A man with a white shirt on with an orange tie and black trousers stepped in. He cleared his throat and said, "Maximus wants to see you. He said I'm suppose to teach maths today."

Mr Slake looked so annoyed he might go on a violent rampage then blow up. "FINE!" Then he strolled out of the classroom like nothing had happened.

The man looked a bit happier now as he walked towards the whiteboard.

"Er...hello children. My name is Mr Yurt, and I may well be your new maths teacher!" he said writing his name on the board.

"What are you doing there young man?" He asked Frank. Frank replied, "er..Nothing!" and sat back down.

"Right, OK. Er...what do you normally do?" Mr Yurt asked.

"Nothing," Peter said, lying.

"Well, we normally do some maths questions," Lucy said, frowning.

"OK, oh – I nearly forgot! Firstly - would anyone like to take something to Mr Cuewant's office?" Mr Yurt said.

Frank's hand shot up; he wanted to see Mr Slake getting sacked. Mr Yurt passed a small sheet of paper folded up and then he opened the classroom's door for Frank. As soon as he heard the door shut, he broke into a run. Surprisingly, not one person came across Frank and stopped him; he was still looking out for Shadrik though. He hadn't seen him since he chased Mr Slake down the corridor; Frank didn't actually know what he did at the school, maybe he was the caretaker. Frank then skidded himself to a stop when he landed outside of Mr Cuewant's office. He could hear a muttered conversation being exchanged but when he got closer to the door, he could hear more clearly. Frank peeked through a small window and saw Mr Slake and Mr Cuewant, both standing up, talking.

"Luke, I trusted you. Did you not think I wouldn't read the paper?" Mr Cuewant asked calmly.

"I did, yes. But, you did, you let Frank go when he climbed over the fence!" Mr Slake answered.

"He did not climb over the fence, it's too high!" (Frank felt a bit less worried now as Mr Cuewant believed him). "And anyway, I do not care what you said about Frank, but you told that 'reporter' none of the teachers like me, is this true?" Mr Cuewant said.

"What?! Of course not!" Slake said.

"How come he quoted you saying it then? You also said you'd be happy when I leave. I don't think I can trust you anymore, Luke." Mr Cuewant said sitting down.

"No, you can. I can change! Please!" Slake begged.

"But will you? You called me stupid and an absolute idiot, why did you say that?"

"I - I didn't mean to say that! They made me!" Slake said trying to sound innocent.

"They didn't though, they didn't force you to say anything! And if they did, it's cowardly of you to say it anyway. What did they do to you, hold a knife to your throat?" Mr Cuewant said looking towards the door.

Frank ducked down but he was sure Mr Cuewant had seen him.

"No, I – well...er..." Frank could tell Mr Slake was trying really hard to think of an excuse.

"You leave me no choice, Luke!" Mr Cuewant said very calmly, he was not moving at all, still as a statue.

"No, look, I'll make it up to you, Maximus! You know I've always admired you…!" he said sycophantically.

"I'm sorry, Luke. I can't trust you, you're-" Mr Cuewant was interrupted by Mr Slake's begging.

"Please don't say it - dear Maximus…!"

"Luke, You're Sacked! End Of! I expect you to clear your belongings out of your room as soon as possible. Thank you." And he stood up.

This was the perfect time to knock on the door, so he did.

"Yes, come in." Mr Cuewant said.

Frank opened the door and saw Mr Slake stare at him with a well practised scrutiny that was designed to intimidate.

"Er...Mr Yort our new maths teacher - said to hand this to you, sir." Frank said.

"Yurt, OK," Mr Cuewant said taking the piece of paper out of his hand. "You may leave, both of you. No more questions."

Mr Slake looked disgusted, "Maximus," he begged.

"I said no more questions, Luke. Out!" Mr Cuewant said.

He slammed the door shut and turned to Frank; who was now halfway down the corridor as he knew what Slake would do if he got hold of him because he was now sacked. Frank could not wait to tell Peter that Mr Slake had been sacked...

"He's sacked! Slake!" Frank said happily as he sat next to Peter. "I witnessed the whole thing!"

"Thank God for that! Would that mean you don't get detention after school?" Peter asked.

"If Mr Yurt doesn't find out!" Frank whispered.

Peter smirked and concentrated back on the lesson.

Chapter 13- Christmas Day

It was Christmas Eve and Frank was lying on his bed, looking up at the ceiling dreamily. He wasn't excited for the next day as he knew he'd only get a pair of odd socks from his grandparents and he wouldn't have any Christmas lunch. The past few weeks had been boring but a bit happier as Mr Slake had been sacked. Sam the suspected vampire had still not turned up at school as far as Frank knew, and Peter was now obsessed with him. Mr Yurt had brightened up his new classroom a bit more - well a lot more compared to how drab it had looked when it was Slake's - and he didn't give Frank detention if he was five seconds late. In fact, the only time Frank had detention since Mr Slake's time was when it was Art with Mrs Rose; she still had not been sacked yet. She'd been acting a bit weirder than usual over the past few weeks, she'd been doing things like: writing Snilbog on the whiteboard, drinking from a small flask a lot, and picking on Frank especially. Frank had heard nothing from Teethy or Frangini since the dragon incident. There had been three football matches since September and the league table, which was on the board outside Mr Yurt's classroom looked like this:

1. *Lions 6 points*

2. *Snakes 1 point*

3. *Scorpions 1 point*

Through the shed window he could see the starry night sky was scattered with millions of bright stars which made it look magical. Frank was very tired so he turned over and tried to get to sleep. It was only eight o'clock when Frank actually fell asleep, the only sounds coming into the shed were the distant howlings of the local dogs.

****

BEEP! BEEP! BEEP! Frank opened his eyes and saw something terrifying. Two large eyes were a centimetre away from Frank's. "Hello Mr Frank!" the creature squeaked.

"Teethy? What are you doing here?" Frank yawned.

Teethy was wearing some scruffy old robes which were made out of green coloured curtains.

"Teethy has come-"

BEEP! BEEP! BEEP! BANG! Teethy had just whacked the alarm clock with a hammer and it was now broken into bits on the floor.

"Teethy! What are you-"

"Teethy has come to drop presents off at Mr Frank's, Mr Peter's and Miss Lucy's house! Teethy has brought you this!" Teethy said holding out a new alarm clock!

"Oh, thank you, Teethy! Just what I need!...Now! Er...I got you something as well!" Frank lied. He pulled out a small

176

blue jumper from his clothes drawers, when he was four it had fitted him but it didn't anymore.

"Thank you, Mr Frank!" Teethy squeaked, and quickly threw off his scruffy robes and put the jumper on over his head, struggling a bit when his long nose wouldn't fit through the neck, when he finally got it on it went down to his knees!

"Thank you, Mr Frank!" He kept saying, as he climbed up to look at himself in the mirror.

"Teethy looks very smart now Mr Frank!"

"So, have you been to Peter's and Lucy's houses yet?" Frank asked, hiding a smile behind his hand at Teethy's reaction and antics.

"Oh, yes!" Teethy squeaked. "Apple and the other elves have given you some presents as well as Teethy!"

Frank couldn't believe it! He had presents! At the foot of his bed were lots of different presents all wrapped in weird wrapping paper.

"I – you – thank you!" Frank was nonplussed by the amount of small, medium and large presents there were.

"And, Mr Frank, would Mr Frank like to come for Christmas dinner at the Elf Chamber?" Teethy asked.

"What? Oh, yeh, yeh! Sure would! Deffo!" Frank was flabbergasted.

"Oh, good, good, good! Mr Frank can open his presents now!" Teethy squealed with delight; and so he did.

The presents that the Elves had given him were things like: bright coloured socks, weird coloured floppy hats, some blank pieces of paper, some pictures of the Elf that sent it, some thick books about famous Elves and chocolate bars! Teethy then muttered something under his breath and he grabbed Frank's arm. BANG! They had just transported from the shed to the heart of the Elf Chamber!

"Er...Teethy, what was that ward or spell that you said at the shed?"

"Teethy put an invisible ward on the presents so other humans can't see them!" Teethy said.

Then Frank realised he wasn't in the middle of the cave. He was only at the side of the cave, he had a stupendous view of an immense Christmas tree which was in the centre of the chamber. It had decorations all over it with a big golden star at the top, it nearly touched the ceiling of the cave and as the Elves were generally no taller than Frank's hips he didn't know how they could have managed to get up to the top of it.

"Er...Teethy what shall I do until lunch time?" Frank said looking around at the deserted cave.

"Explore! Mr Peter and Miss Lucy are not coming! See you at Christmas Dinner! -Bye" Teethy then turned around and ran up the tower's staircase.

So Frank did as Teethy had suggested and he had a good walk and look around this amazing place. It was five minutes to twelve when he got back to where he'd started, just as Frangini was coming down the staircase.

"Only six hours late!" Frangini laughed. "Come on, time for Christmas Dinner! ELVES - MAKE THE TABLE!" He bellowed.

Just like every other time Frank had had a meal there, the Elves' hands were filled with blocks of foam after a couple of seconds. In what seemed like a nanosecond, the table had been made and once again two large seats had been set up for Frank and Frangini. The Elves then ran down into the kitchen and appeared again – but this time with their hands full of plates piled up with Christmas Dinner food!

"SIT!" bellowed Frangini.

Immediately, the Elves, along with Frank, sat down at the table. Frangini was limping a bit, as he was very old, he got to the table and sat down, "HELLO ELVES! MERRY CHRISTMAS TO ALL OF YOU. THANK YOU FOR ALL OF YOUR WONDERFUL GIFTS! LET THE FEAST...BEGIN!"

Before anyone else's, Frank's plate was filled with: chicken, beef, stuffing, peas, carrots, Yorkshire pudding, pigs in blankets, roast potatoes, sprouts and gravy. His plate was also empty before anyone else's!

"Wow, you gobbled that down quickly!" Frangini said while stuffing a roast potato into his mouth.

"I was really hungry," Frank mumbled. He couldn't move because of how full he was.

"It's half- twelve already! Better get on with pudding. TIME FOR PUDDING!" Frangini bellowed.

The Elves walked this time towards the kitchen and it took them at least ten seconds to emerge from it due to them all being stuffed with Christmas dinner as well!

"COME ON, CHOP CHOP! HURRY UP!"

The table was set again with mainly bowls and spoons. There were puddings like: Christmas pudding, custard, cake and, well that was really it. Frank got a bowl of custard and a slab of chocolate fudge cake and sat there for half an hour just breaking it down into crumbs and forcing them into his mouth. When lunch had finished, Frank decided he'd go back to his shed and just lie in a food stuffed stupor on his bed.

"That was fantastic! Best Christmas Dinner I've ever had! Thank you very much, thank you all very much! Can I go back home now?" Frank asked Frangini who was now half- asleep.

"Huh, what? Oh, yeh, sure, Teethy!" Frangini yawned.

Teethy appeared from nowhere the moment his name was called out.

"Yes, Master?"

"Would you take Frank back to his shed house?" Frangini mumbled.

"OK, Master," Teethy said and then he touched Frank's arm and they disappeared from the scene.

A second later they were back in the shed.

"Thanks, Teethy, thanks a lot! Bye," Frank said.

Teethy then disappeared in a circle of coloured wind and then the only sound in the shed was Frank's breathing. He turned around so he was facing the window and was amazed when he saw a magical sight. Snow covered the trees and houses of Candlestick street and Frank was almost buried in it when he stepped outside. Frank didn't have any plans for the afternoon except for lying on his bed stuffed and reading his book, but he decided to first take a little walk into the forest where he had first met the Elves.

He put on his thick, woolly coat that Parry had given him, then his warm, red gloves Apple had given him and put his new green and yellow bobble hat on Frangini had given him during lunch; he then opened the door and set off for his walk.

The snowing had stopped by now and the vast forest was silent and deserted. There were lots of things lingering in Frank's mind including: Mrs Rose's weird actions, Slake's sacking, Sam Matthews and what dangerous event would he have to tackle next. *Either she just doesn't like me and she's weird or she's been possessed or something* Frank thought (about Mrs Rose). *I'll tell Mr Cuewant about her as soon as I get back to school.* Frank then heard muttered conversations in the trees to his left. The voices sounded familiar so he moved cautiously through the snow towards where they were coming from. Frank poked his head between two large oak trees and saw who was talking: Mr Cuewant and Frangini.

"Olivier, you know what will happen, don't you?" Mr Cuewant hissed.

"It's just a coincidence, Maximus. Don't worry!" said Frangini.

"But it's not! Don't you know what this means? These events aren't just coincidences! These signs, it means something!" Mr Cuewant said.

"What signs? What events? It's nothing, Maximus!" Frangini reassured.

"What signs? The snake at the Spelling Bee! The force stopping us when Frank was alone with the dragon! Something wanted Frank dead! They all mean something, they have to! It means he'll return sooner or later – but he will return though! And he'll kill everything that moves that's not part of his army! We need to prepare!" Mr Cuewant said nervously.

Frangini looked down at his feet and bit his lip.

"Yeh, but, maybe..."

"He will return! He's got so many vicious followers! If he wants you dead, you're dead. They'll torture and murder you in the most painful way possible! You have to listen to me, Olivier!" Mr Cuewant said.

"OK! Are you sure?" Frangini asked.

"I'm sure!" Mr Cuewant said and he disappeared in a flurry of coloured wind.

Frangini then did the same, and left Frank disoriented. Questions were flying into his head, *who would return? King Goblin? Does something want me dead? Who would torture and murder you in the most painful way possible? Goblins?* Frank walked as quick as he could through the knee deep snow, back to his shed, bed and book, trying to understand what he had just heard.

Chapter 14- Doluffid Potion

Nearly six months had passed by, and Frank had still not told Mr Cuewant about Mrs Rose's strange and unexplained writing incidents on the whiteboard in the classroom that had started just before last Christmas, and she'd done similar strange writings several times since then as well. Sometimes her behaviour was really odd as well, odd and sometimes a bit scary. Now it was drawing nearer and nearer to the Summer holidays. It was on the last week of the school year when Mrs Rose's behaviour finally convinced Frank to go to Mr Cuewant and tell him all about what had been happening. It was the last Monday of the term (and the last art lesson) when Mrs Rose was talking about graffiti. She said the words: *'and because it is the last lesson of this wondrous school year...'* and then she just stopped in the middle of the sentence. She took really deep breaths and ran towards her desk; she then acted like she was trying to find something important. Mrs Rose chucked nearly everything on her desk onto the floor and then picked up a small flask and drank from it for about twenty seconds.

"Oh - Class dismissed!" Mrs Rose told them, then sighed with pleasure before drinking from the flask again.

When everyone had gathered all their things together and were walking out, staring at her, she just ignored them and carried on glugging down whatever was in the flask.

"I'm going to Mr Cuewant's office," Frank told Peter and

Lucy as he broke out of the crowd.

The classrooms were still full and when Frank walked past Mr Solte's (a tall man with a mostly bald head with wiry hair sprouting out around the sides) classroom, he saw Shadrik on the field watering some large plants, talking to Mr Johnson.

He arrived at Mr Cuewant's office door. Knock, knock.

"Come in!"

Frank carefully opened the door and found Mr Cuewant with his hands resting on the table.

"Is this the fiftieth or sixtieth time this term you've been in here? What've you got to tell me this time Frank?" Mr Cuewant laughed.

"Er..." Frank didn't know what to start with. "I- er...well Mrs Rose has been acting kinda strange, and I was wondering if you'd tell me what's wrong with her?"

Mr Cuewant narrowed his eyes at Frank, "And, er...what strange events have been happening in Mrs Rose's class?" he asked brushing his hair back from his temples.

"Well, she keeps on being weird," Frank's mind had gone blank; Mr Cuewant was still staring at him curiously.

"But what is she doing that's weird?" Mr Cuewant was now getting a bit impatient.

"She, er...today she said something about school ending and

she started chucking everything off her desk. Then she picked up a flask and started to drink from it, then she let us out!" Frank said.

Mr Cuewant looked nervous now, "Has anything else been happening?" he asked.

"Well, yeh, for the past six months she keeps on writing Snilbog on the-"

"I knew it! I knew it! Why didn't you tell me earlier? I told him these signs meant something! I told him! Er...when did this start?" Mr Cuewant said.

"Since the start of the school year," Frank said.

"Frank, haven't you noticed? 'Snilbog'?" Mr Cuewant asked, "right - just stay here!"

He ran out of the room and down the corridor, leaving Frank bewildered. He sat in the chair opposite Mr Cuewant's and waited. Thirty seconds later, the headmaster came back into the room and hissed to Frank, "Quick! Get behind the door!"

So he did. The corridor was silent and vacant for a few seconds then Frank heard footsteps walking down it. The footsteps got louder and louder and then stopped. Mr Cuewant was flapping his hand at Frank to signal him to get further along the wall.

Mrs Rose then walked in and without any warning she was taken onto the floor by Mr Cuewant who did a martial arts sleeper hold on her. Frank's mouth was slightly open but his eyes were wide at the sight of the Headmaster taking down one of the teachers he hated most so quickly and skilfully! Mrs Rose was still breathing but she was not moving. Mr Cuewant lifted her up and chucked her onto the chair Frank had been sitting on just a few moment ago.

"Frank, get that rope and pass it to me!" Mr Cuewant commanded pointing towards a piece of curled up rope on the window sill. Frank gave the long, thick piece of rope to Mr Cuewant who then expertly tied the rope around Mrs Rose's hands and then round and round the chair.

"I just hope she is what I think she is or I'll be in big trouble Frank," he said.

At that moment, Mrs Rose woke up.

"NO! YOU! - You've found the secret! Who told you? IT WAS HIM WASN'T IT?!" Mrs Rose shrieked pointing towards Frank.

The bell to signal break time rang and Mrs Rose carried on shrieking above it.

"Frank, would you - SHUT UP MRS ROSE! - OR WHATEVER YOU ARE! - Sorry about that, would you get that bottle of water on my desk please?"

Frank turned around and saw a red bottle with a blue label on it that read, '*Doluffid Potion*' on Mr Cuewant's desk. He picked it up and gave it to Mr Cuewant who gave it back to Frank. Mr Cuewant went behind Mrs Rose, grabbed her head and tilted it backwards, holding her jaw open at the same time. He told Frank, "Quick - Pour it in! Pour it into her mouth!"

After he'd done that, Mr Cuewant stepped towards Frank and pulled him over to the other side of the desk. Mrs Rose's head fell forwards and then it came back up slowly from her chest, her eyes were now turning black...

"Yep, the Doluffid Potion never fails!" Mr Cuewant said looking down at the flask that had just fallen out of her pocket - the one that she had been frantically drinking out of in class earlier.

"This creature took Rebecca's DNA and put it into a drink, it then drank it, and it turned into, or cloned itself into a copy of her for several months at a time everytime it drank it - and it's hidden the real Rebecca – Mrs Rose, somewhere!"

By the time he was finished talking, it wasn't Mrs Rose... sitting in the seat now was a creature unlike anything Frank had never seen; it was a bit bigger than an Elf and had green scaly skin. It had two sharp pointed horns, one on each side of its bald head that were a paler green, and it had had an ugly smile leering at them on it's cruel face. It's demonic eyes were black.

"It's Yashin," Mr Cuewant whispered sinisterly. "You're Snilbog's most faithful servant, aren't you?"

"Yes, it is me! And Yes I am," the creature said and then it let out a nightmarish laugh, its foul breath made Frank's nose wrinkle in disgust.

"You've murdered so many people. Now, I am going to ask you two things, Yashin. Have you finally murdered Rebecca Rose, and where is she?" Mr Cuewant said.

"Key secret room," Yashin muttered.

"I will make sure you are punished for centuries for doing this!" Mr Cuewant said.

"I don't think so!" Yashin cackled mockingly at him.

Just then, the creature's arms broke the rope twisted round him as easily as it would brush away a cobweb, and held out his hands, sending a beam of energy which made Mr Cuewant and Frank fly backwards in the air and crash into the back wall, then slump together onto the floor. Yashin stood up, walked to the office door, turned around and let out a roar of wicked laughter – whilst clapping his hands - and disappeared in a puff of green smoke that smelt like rotten eggs! He'd gone in the same way as Sam had in the Elf Chamber all those weeks ago!

"I'm going to start searching for Rebecca," Mr Cuewant said whilst getting up from the floor.

"I think I know where she is," Frank said.

Mr Cuewant looked stunned. "Show me," he whispered; and Frank led the way.

He took him to Mrs Rose's office and got her chair. He placed it next to the wall, stood on it and looked through the window into the tiny room that he had first seen Mrs Rose in. Just like he expected, the real Mrs Rose was sitting in the corner.

"She's in there," Frank said.

Mr Cuewant had just rummaged through a drawer in the desk and pulled out a small, golden key. He walked towards the wall Frank had propped the chair against and pushed the key into a cleverly disguised key hole. A handle appeared out of nowhere and Mr Cuewant turned it; a part of the wall opened up leaving space for him to go inside. Frank didn't know if he should go charging in or to just see what Mr Cuewant did, he decided to just watch what the Headmaster was doing. Mrs Rose was talking and Mr Cuewant was speaking through a walkie-talkie he'd pulled out of a pocket in his jacket..

"Quickly! She's almost insane!" he was saying into it.

"IT WAS HIM! YASHIN! TORTURE! ME! HE SAW ME!" Mrs Rose screamed pointing at Frank. "I'LL KILL YOU! I WILL! YOU SAW ME! YOU DIDN'T SAVE ME! YASHIN! HE TORTURED ME!"

"Frank, just ignore her!" Mr Cuewant shouted over her screams.

"YOU'RE GOING TO DIE! HE TOLD ME! NATAS SNILBOG WILL RISE ONCE MORE! HE TOLD ME!"

"QUICKLY! COME ON, QUICKLY!" Mr Cuewant was now shouting to someone on the walkie-talkie.

This was mayhem! Just then, Mr Feather, Mr Solte, Miss Abs, Shadrik, Mr Johnson, both of the Olfankos's and Miss Fragantank (the geography teacher) came running into the room. Mr Solte put himself in front of Frank as Mrs Rose was trying to escape from Mr Cuewant's arms. After five minutes of battling with Mrs Rose, Miss Fragantank, Shadrik and Mr Johnson took her out of the office; she still hadn't stopped screaming and shouting.

"She's insane, she's going to St Plange's!" Mr Cuewant sighed. "My office, now Frank!"

Frank was horrified at what he'd just witnessed. He ran down the corridor wanting to get away from it all, and he waited outside the office for Mr Cuewant to catch up.

"Come in and sit down Frank," Mr Cuewant said.

"Er...what was that thing?"

"That, my friend, was a goblin. A particularly nasty Goblin. When Snilbog was at his most powerful, Yashin was his ever faithful lackey. When Snilbog, well...er...disappeared, some say that Yashin still does undercover work for his master. This is, what I suspect what happened, last year sometime, when Yashin targeted and caught Rebecca. He tortured her which sent her insane. Instead of killing her though, he decided to send her even more insane by locking her in that secret room for a year. How did he change into her? I bet your next question will be? Well, he drank a magical potion he'd made and mixed in to it her DNA samples that he'd got from her body when he tortured her. And so, he was able to clone himself into a copy of her. That's why he had to keep drinking that, Doluffid Potion, as it's called to maintain his new appearance." Mr Cuewant explained patiently..

But Frank was still confused. There was a brief moment of silence and then Mr Solte came in, "They're here - the Plange vans to take her away," he said and then walked back down the corridor.

"Plange vans?" Frank asked, even more confused!

"St Plange is a hospital for the mentally insane, and they will be their vans to take her there." Mr Cuewant said walking over to the window and looking down at the white vans with *PHMI* in red written in big, bold writing on them that were outside.

"Why do they need three vans?" asked Frank, joining him.

"They must think she's dangerous, the other two will be full of special security staff." Mr Cuewant said.

Peter and Lucy then appeared at the door.

"What happened? Are you alright?" Lucy asked running towards Frank.

"Mrs Rose was turned into a goblin! Her real body was locked in a secret room and now she's dangerously insane so

192

she's going to a hospital for mentally deranged people," Frank told her.

"Oh dear, poor Mrs Rose! - Are you alright though?" Lucy asked nervously.

"Yeh, I'm OK, I think!" Frank answered.

"So she was a goblin?" said Peter quickly.

"Yeh, well - no! Well sort of! It was a goblin called Yashin who made himself look like her...I think."

"Is that why she – it - it kept writing *Snilbog* on the whiteboard and acting weird?" asked Lucy.

"Yep, that's why – wait! What's happening outside?" Frank asked remembering that it had just been break time.

"They're staying out until lunch, they told us," Peter said.

"Who told you?"

"Solte and Abs."

There was an awkward silence and then Peter asked, "Er...have you...er...seen Mr Slake lately, Mr Cuewant?" Frank smirked.

"Luke? No, I don't know where he is actually, he cleared out his office and left without a word!" Mr Cuewant said.

"Oh, this might sound weird but...maybe he's planning like revenge," Frank said. "It's obvious, isn't it? He never liked you and now he'll have a massive grudge against you!"

"Yeah, but Luke isn't like that, he wouldn't harm anyone!" Mr Cuewant said.

Frank looked at Peter and Lucy who had raised their eyebrows slightly in surprise on hearing that, and they had 'Yeah, right' looks on their faces.

"So who are the new teachers for next term going to be Mr Cuewant?" asked Peter.

"Well, I get to decide who's doing what but I just won't be here next term. I've not got anyone in mind yet, I'll have to have to put my thinking cap on, won't I? "Right, let's all go outside."

Frank led the way but when he touched the door, something happened. It felt like he was being transported somewhere, the room just disappeared and...**THUMP!** He landed with both feet on hard ground, and then he felt Mr Cuewant land, and stagger into him on his knees...

Chapter 15- Slake's Revenge

Frank opened his eyes. He and Mr Cuewant were in a strange place, but it didn't feel like it was an underground chamber or anything like that, but it was hard to tell as it was really dark. They were stood on and a pathway made out of stone slabs which stretched away from them to their left and right. What little light there was came from a flaming torch fixed into the wall close by behind them. Frank turned around and then he saw that they were actually on – and very close to - the edge of a high cliff!. He couldn't make out what was at the bottom as all he saw was darkness.

He dropped a large stone and waited; *one second, two seconds, three seconds, four seconds, five seconds,* **BANG!** The stone had taken five seconds to hit the bottom of the cliff.

"Frank Burray, how nice to see you!" a voice whispered.

"Shut it!" Frank knew whose voice that was.

He spun around and saw the man he had hated all year round; he had on his usual black, mouldy cape and tight black trousers. His hair was lank and greasy...the man who now had a long curved knife to Mr Cuewant's throat was...Mr Slake.

"Luke, please, *what do you think you're doing?!* What do you want?" muttered Mr Cuewant.

"HA HA!" he bellowed, "NOW you're asking what I want! Eh?! You sacked me! Now I want...REVENGE! REVENGE!

And I'm going to have it!"

"Wait, wait, wait - why though?" Frank asked nervously looking over to what looked like the inside of Mr Cuewant's office door at one end of the path, about a room length away, and hoping for it to open and someone come in and help them.

Mr Cuewant asked him the same question.

"WHY? YOU DARE ASK ME WHY?! IT'S BECAUSE! Its because - you never liked me or listened to me, did you Maximus? ARE YOU LISTENING TO ME NOW?" Slake shouted. "Why didn't you ever listen to me before?"

"I did! I trusted you! I hired you because I trusted you, but you gave me no choice! - I had to sack you! Now please, look - I'll let you have your job back if you just lower the knife," Mr Cuewant said desperately..

"OH NO! HA HA! No no NO! My revenge is that you will die and I'll leave Frank Burray here to starve! Nobody and nothing can save you now!" Slake laughed like a maniac. "I will get my revenge, now..."

The door Frank had seen banged open and both the Olfankos, Mr Solte, Miss Abs and Shadrik all stood in the doorway.

"*NO!*" Slake cried out seeing them as witnesses to what he was about to do. He let go of Mr Cuewant's throat and put his hand over his eyes shaking his head for a moment, but he still held the long curved knife in his other hand...

Mr Cuewant leaped away from Slake and loudly shouted out, "CAREFUL! HE'S GOT A KNIFE!" To warn the ones who had just appeared and were rushing forwards..

"He has?" Miss Abs cried out nervously, stopping suddenly, her gold rimmed glasses slipping down her nose..

"GO BACK, I'LL HANDLE HIM NOW!" Mr Cuewant roared.

"*NO!* We'll help you with him Maximus," Shadrik shouted.

"WELL COME ON THEN! STOP FAFFING ABOUT!"

Mr Solte, Ravius and Shadrik came running forwards, leaving the ladies jumping from side to side frantically as if the floor was boiling lava. Mr Slake was now running stupidly towards the other end of the cliff edge, even though it looked like it was a dead end. Soon enough, just like Frank had expected, Slake was cornered by the four male teachers.

"Are you alright?" Mr Solte muttered to Mr Cuewant.

"Yes, Andy, I'm alright."

"Look, Luke. Just give us the knife and no-one gets hurt!" Ravius said glancing at the long curved knife that Slake was now waving around in front of him, which stopped them from getting any closer to him.

"And what will you give me back in return?" Slake smirked smugly.

"Nothing, like I said, just give us the knife and no-one gets hurt!" Ravius said.

"Never!" Shrieked Slake as he lunged quickly forward and tried to stab Mr Cuewant in the chest, but he kicked out and the knife went deep into his leg, snarling with rage Slake pulled it out and positioned himself to attack again. Miss Abs and Heather screamed hysterically when Slake then threw the knife at Mr Cuewant, but he quickly ducked and it just missed him.

"MAXIMUS!" cried Heather.

Mr Slake let out a sudden roar of maddened frustration whilst stepping backwards, but he obviously hadn't realised that a large rock was just behind his knees – and it caused him to topple over the cliff edge

"HELP! PLEASE!" His shouts and piercing cries died down and then a loud **THUMP** signalled that he had just hit the bottom. Without any doubt he was dead, nobody could survive a fall like that. There was no further sound coming from below.

Frank hadn't realised Mr Slake had toppled over the cliff as the teachers blocked his view, but he knew something had happened as the teachers were now looking down over the edge, but there was no sign of Slake.

"Where's Mr Slake gone?" He shouted out to them.

"Dead, gone, toppled down, fell to his death!" Ravius said.

Mr Cuewant started yelling as the pain from his stab wound suddenly started. Shadrik poured some water from his watering can (Frank was wondering the same thing, he didn't know why he had a watering can) onto the wound on his leg.

"Luke's dead, Maximus," Shadrik said, this is my special growing water, it helps the plants to grow quick – I was watering them in the corridor plant pots before – it'll help your leg to heal quicker...".

They all helped to lift Mr Cuewant up and he started limping towards the far door leaning onto Shadrik, "Thanks Shadrik, thanks to you all – for a moment back there I thought…." he said his voice suddenly very shaky.

"I'll take Frank back, I can't believe Luke jinxed the door to ambush us – and he really meant to kill us!" Mr Cuewant said, anger taking over from shakiness in his voice, "come on Frank."

Frank, with the Headmaster limping alongside him, walked from the scene of Slake's attack. They were quickly back in the office.

"Where were you?" Lucy asked.

Frank wasn't listening, he was helping the limping Mr Cuewant towards his seat. The headmaster sat down heavily and taking deep breaths.

"Mr Cuewant...are you alright? Frank, what happened?"

Peter said.

"Slake, he's, he's..."

"He's dead," Mr Cuewant interrupted.

"What, you saw it?" Lucy whispered.

"Well, when we disappeared from here – Slake had jinxed the door - we turned up on a cliff edge, Slake was waiting for us and he held a long knife to Mr Cuewant's throat, he was going to kill him, then the other teachers came, cornered Slake, he stabbed Mr Cuewant in the leg, then threw the knife at him, then he toppled off the cliff, and fell to his death, we came back, that's a short summary of what happened." Frank said trying to be nonchalant but they could tell he was a bit shocked..

An ambulance arrived at the front of the school and two paramedics from them came running up into Mr Cuewant's office, "We got the call that you'd been stabbed in the leg", one of them with a big beard stated, plonking his huge medical bag on the floor.

"Go home, Frank – Peter – Lucy - I'll be back tomorrow," Mr Cuewant muttered, "it's not that bad, and I'm in good hands now."

Then they heard police car sirens screeching into the school grounds.

"Go on Get out, now, before they get in here!"

They left in an instant, dashing down the corridor. Frank thought, *I wonder what lies will be in the Severor Sun this week, probably: MASS MURDERER MAXIMUS CUEWANT KILLS ANOTHER VICTIM, THIS TIME IT WAS THE NICE AND KIND LUKE SLAKE!*

"What a day!" Peter said walking out of the school, as the policemen dashed past them.

"Shut up! 'What a day'! How is it a 'what a day'? Peter, Frank has seen and been through so much today! Why do you think he's not talking?" Lucy said crossly; it was true, Frank hadn't talked since they left Mr Cuewant's office. "He's witnessed a real goblin, an insane person saying that she'll kill him, Mr Slake trying to kill Mr Cuewant and him and then Mr Slake killed himself…!"

"He didn't kill himself, he slipped off the edge, then died," Frank murmured.

"Oh, well c'mon then!" Lucy said.

"Hang on, where we going?" Peter asked.

"That forest we first met the Elves in, I've found something that might interest you - and I'm not telling you, Peter," Lucy said bossily realising that Peter was about to ask something; he didn't speak after that.

When they got to the forest, it didn't look as magical as it had done when it had been covered in snow. The sun was shining brightly in the blue sky, the grass was green and there were a few muddy puddles here and there. The trees' branches had grown and looked like long muscular arms, and every time Frank walked between two, they caught him and he had to escape from their claws. But nothing strange happened, it was all quite normal, and everything was quiet.

"Nearly there, not far now," Lucy whispered, "keep quiet!"

"Where exactly-"

"Peter, shut up!" Lucy hissed.

"OK, OK!" Peter smirked towards Frank.

After five more minutes of walking in silence, Lucy brought them to a stop. Frank was astonished when he looked through two large bushes and saw a boy he'd been longing to see...Sam Matthews. He was crouching with a jumper and shorts on, then Lucy picked up a flapping piece of paper reading:

MISSING

SAM MATTHEWS

It had a photo of Sam's face at the bottom.

"He's missing?" Peter whispered.

"Yep, well, he was – but *I* found him yesterday!," Lucy smugly said to them.

Sam looked up suddenly and stared at Frank, Peter and Lucy. He hissed really loudly, quickly got to his feet and ran away from them through the trees..

"C'mon, we have to go after him!" Frank said running after him.

Peter and Lucy ran after him, but after a minute of running, Frank had got well ahead of them, they caught upto him in the middle of the forest, breathing deeply, and looking around.

"I lost him," Frank panted.

"We lost- HE'S THERE!" Peter bellowed, pointing his arm out over to their left.

Indeed, Sam Matthews was running down a small, muddy path between the trees. This time, they all ran after him together, Sam just kept on running. Past a big pool of muddy water...through some twisted trees...jumping over some massive tree trunks that had been blown over – it was all like an army assault course!

Then...*SPLAT!* Frank, Peter and Lucy had all just tripped over a long fallen branch and gone face-first into a heap of mud the main trunk had churned up..

"Where's...er…Sam...he's gone...urgh! I...can't see...but I can smell stuff, and it's not nice stuff...!" Peter said wiping the sticky mud off his face.

Frank, was standing up scraping and shaking the mud off

him, and all he could see were trees close by all around them. Peter and Lucy were both just about covered from head to toe in mud and were slowly getting up from their knees. Sam, however was nowhere to be seen.

"Where's he gone?" Peter moaned brushing bits of mud out of his hair.

"I'm up here..." They heard Sam shout.

Sam was high up in the leafy shade of a huge oak tree, sitting on a long branch growing out of its wide trunk.

"SAM? IS THAT YOU? Yep! - It is that's Sam!" Frank said looking up at him.

Just then, an unnaturally strong wind hit the tree Sam was on shaking it fiercely.

Sam was blown off the branch and fell backwards crashing through the lower branches onto the forest floor. Lucy had screamed hysterically when he fell, but Frank and Peter just stood there, paralysed with shock. They quickly recovered and ran over to him. Sam wasn't moving at first but then he twitched and opened his eyes.

"Sam, are you alright?" Lucy and Peter both cried out looking down at him with concern.

Sam didn't answer. But he did hold both his hands up and hiss at them. There was a pause and then a flash of red light came out of his hands, making the two of them fly backwards.

Lucy and Peter both slammed into a tree which made their heads ring and they groaned in pain. Sam, however, had got up and was running away again!

"Frank, go, run! Catch up to him! We're OK! We'll follow in a minute!" Lucy shouted.

Frank started to run after him. Sam was at least twelve metres ahead of him, but something was encouraging him. *Come on! Run! Look - he's slowing down!* And indeed he was. *GO NOW!* Frank ran as fast as he could and before long, he had caught up with him. Strangely, Sam was standing still, staring at Frank. Sam was standing in the shadows of a deep and muddy hole; Frank recognised it as the same one they had used to get through into the Elf Chamber.

"Sam...?" Frank asked nervously.

He didn't answer. Frank stepped down into the hole and was face to face with the pale Sam Matthews. Just then he felt a hot ray of sunshine on the back of his neck. Sam fearfully looked up at the strong sunlight filtering through the trees, panic now in his eyes. It was his eyes that Frank saw change first – they were turning all white, then his legs started wobbling like he'd got a cramp spasm. A second after the sun's rays touched him he was on the floor howling with pain.

"Sam! What's wrong? What can I do?!" Frank shouted.

Then he realised. The sun must be destroying him; Peter was right - he *was* a vampire! Sam's face was turning even paler than usual and he was going wild tearing his green Snake shirt into pieces. He grabbed at Frank's leg who jumped backwards in fright and then kept his distance from the writhing body on the floor. But it was a body that was slowly disappearing...as Frank watched in horror the legs went first, then the arms...the body...the head...and then all that was Sam had gone...but left in the place where Sam had just been writhing was an ash grey rock the size of a tennis ball…

Chapter 16- The Tonkfar and the Hospital

Frank stared at the stone where Sam had been.. Peter was right! He hadn't been imagining things about Sam like Frank had believed him to be doing after all! But what should he do with the stone lying in front of him? Bury it? Leave it? Just then something, a voice, a thought, came into his head...*the stone, the stone, it has to be destroyed in the Elf Chamber, in the Diamond Tonkfar!* He knew then what he had to do... but...there was one thing bugging him. How would he get into the Elf Chamber? Again a thought, a voice, came into his head – *use the password...*

Frank searched his memory, what was it? *I did know it!* Teethy told me! Oh what was it…? Then he suddenly remembered, and in a shaky voice he said out loud, "Eht enots, eht enots, sah ot eb deyortsed ni fle rebmahc, ni eht dnomaid rafknot, Snilbog nos."

It worked! Amazingly Frank was sucked down into the mud somehow without touching it, and he flew down a long slide, the stone clutched in his hands...But there was an unusual bump in the slide – it hadn't been there last time - and when he shot over it, it made him fly up and hit his head on the top of the slide - and he dropped the stone.

"NOOOOOO!" Frank yelled.

The stone tumbled around in the air. Then Frank heard a laugh and a hiss in his ear all at the same time saying, "HA

HA! HE'LL ALWAYS LIVE! IT WILL SMASH AND HE'LL LIVE FOREVER AND DESTROY ANYONE IN HIS WAY! HA HA HA!" The manic laughter got louder echoing down the tunnel slide. "HA HA HA!" the voice then screeched in his ear, "HE WON'T DIE, BUT YOU WILL! YOU STUPID INTERFERING HUMAN BOY! THE STONE WILL NOW SURELY BREAK AND SO THE CURSE WILL STAY ON IT FOR ALL ETERNITY!"

Just then, the tunnel slide levelled off, widened, and grew much higher. Frank scrambled onto his knees and then onto his feet to stand up properly, all the time frantically staring up at the stone that had flown up out of his hand and was now falling...*I can't let it hit the ground*...he leaped up reaching up as high as he could, and just when he got his fingers around it, he fumbled it, lost his balance and fell backwards smacking down onto the hard ground. But very luckily the stone fell onto his chest with a thud and he grabbed it with both hands! He'd got it! Holding it tightly he got up and looked around quickly. The manic laughter from the voice had now turned into a furious wailing - he knew he had to move, get away as quick as possible before - *BANG!* - he was standing about two feet away from the Tonkfar!

The Elves' were all around him around him and they all looked at the stone he was holding to his chest in horror, some even dropping the things that they were carrying. *DO IT, NOW!* That voice in his head was saying. Frank hesitated for a second but then stuck the stone into a small hole where it fitted perfectly in the diamond shape on the front of the Tonkfar.

There was a pause and then a loud BOOM! erupted from the Tonkfar echoing all around the Elf Chamber, which was suddenly plunged into total darkness. *I destroyed it! I did it! Eight lives left!* Frank thought relief washing through him. The chamber started to get brighter as the light returned. Then he heard Frangini's voice shouting, *"FRANK BURRAY! UP IN MY ROOM - NOW!"*

Oh heck! That doesn't sound good! What now?! He stepped past the frightened Elves and walked up the spiral staircase, holding onto the smooth banister rail..

"Oh Good evening Frank," a calm friendly voice said as he walked into Frangini's room. "Do sit down."

Frank went to the seat opposite Frangini's and sat down. A light was turned on and Frangini looked at him intently.

"FRANK, I AM SO HAPPY WITH YOU TODAY! You destroyed an evil object which had deadly curses on it and because you did that our enemy Snilbog is now growing weaker."

"Is that why I heard all the helpful voices in my head at the entrance and in the slide? And how come I transported straight to the Tonkfar?" asked Frank.

"Yes we were sending our voices to you, and Maximus transported you there but had to leave straight away - he's also very proud of you, he wanted me to tell you that!" Frangini said.

"Oh, thanks! But I couldn't've done it without all your help! - It was a Team Effort!" Frank said humbly. "So, what kind of objects are the other Snilbog lives?" he asked.

"Well, obviously, the stone was which now leaves seven. There's a ring hidden somewhere on a little island covered with trees, the sword you found in the Dragon Cave, Snilbog's pet snake - that's the same one that was about to attack you lot at your school during the Spelling Bee, but you can't destroy that yet, a picture you have to burn to destroy, a goblin book-"

"A goblin book?"

Bang! Mr Cuewant appeared, "No, it's a different book from yours," he said, as if reading Frank's mind!

"I'm just naming all the Vouscers to Frank," Frangini told Mr Cuewant.

"Oh there's the sword, the stone," Mr Cuewant said winking at Frank, "the ring, the person who he sees first, his pet, the picture and the book, then the, er..." Frank noticed he was sweating, "and er...the person who killed him first...but, er, anyway, I've come to ask you, Frank, oh - we found Peter and Lucy -" Frank's heart started to beat fast at the way he said that "-and I was wondering if you'd like to pay them a visit at

Scarborough Hospital?"

"Er...What?! The Hospital? What...? Are they hurt, are they...?"

"Don't worry, don't worry! We got to them in time, they're going to be fine! Come on then!" Mr Cuewant then held Frank's arm and they disappeared from Frangini's room and reappeared in some tall bushes outside Scarborough hospital.

It was a large, plain white building and was always packed full of people, last time Frank went there, was when he was five, Grampa Joe 'accidentally' threw a hot cup of tea which fell onto Frank's leg and burnt it, and they had had to wait more than three hours.

Mr Cuewant went straight over to the entrance desk with Frank..

"Names?," a lady with a ponytail in her hair asked them in a bored voice..

"Er...Cuewant and Burray - we're here to see Peter Puginic and Lucy Dart," Mr Cuewant answered.

"Second floor, room twenty-three, it's up there." she said waving her hand to her left, and carried on looking at her computer screen.

Mr Cuewant and Frank took the lift to the second floor and walked down the corridor towards room twenty-three.

"Are...they...OK?" Frank nervously asked.

"Yes, not too bad, all things considered!"

Mr Cuewant opened the wooden doors with *Room Twenty-Three* painted on them and walked in, alongside Frank who just moved his foot in time for the door to swing past him. Frank saw two beds with a large, red curtain between the middle of them, with Peter on the right bed and Lucy on the left. Worryingly they both had bandages wrapped around the top of their heads...Next to Peter there was a skinny man with black hair wearing a pair of white shorts and a green t-shirt, and a large lady with blondish hair, the same as Peters, round glasses, and wearing a bright red dress with large flower patterns on it. On either side of Lucy's bed there was a bald man with dirty sports kit on (shorts and shirt with different coloured paint splodges on it) and a moustache, while on the other side of her, was a skinny lady in denim dungarees and she had long pink hair.

"You must be Frank, I'm Peter's mum, Sandy," the lady in the red flowery dress said in what sounded like to Frank a false posh voice. She was yawning as well whilst shaking his hand but not actually looking at him.

Peter's dad, however, was very enthusiastic about meeting Frank.

"Hello Frank! I'm Peter's dad, Sirius," said the man on Peter's right, shaking Frank's hand hard. "It's a pleasure to meet you, Peter often mentions you!"

"Nice to meet you too, Mr Puginic," Frank said politely..

"Please, call me Sirius," he replied.

"You shall call me Mrs Puginic," Peter's mum said in her posh voice.

"Er...OK," Frank said awkwardly looking down at his feet.

"Mum, shut up!" Peter muttered through his gritted teeth.

"HE..." She pointed accusingly at Frank - "He left you to starve!" Mrs Puginic exclaimed.

"*What?*" Frank gasped!

"I said, young man...-"

"Oh Shut Up, Mum!" Peter said angrily.

"Pleasure to meet you Frank, I'm Lucy's mum, Debbie, and this is Lucy's dad, Gary," the lady Frank hadn't spoken to yet said pointing at herself and the man next to Lucy. "Lucy's always talking about you and Peter."

"Mum, shut up," Lucy groaned in embarrassment..

"Are you looking forward to the summer holidays?" Debbie asked him in a friendly manner, ignoring Lucy.

"Er...yeh, I am, thanks," Frank replied it was a bit of an awkward question: '*are you looking forwards to the summer holidays?*' When his real answer should be – *no not really!*

"Are you two alright?" Frank asked Peter and Lucy.

"Oh I'm sure they'll be fine...parents, would you mind leaving the room?" Mr Cuewant asked kindly, but in his usual blunt way.

"Aren't you Maximus Cuewant, that man we read about in the paper, the one who harms children?" Mrs Puginic asked, in an annoyed posh voice.

"You've been reading the Severor Sun, haven't you?" snapped Mr Cuewant.

"Indeed I have, I find it very interesting and it always let's everyone know the truth of what is happening..." She said this time in a haughty posh voice.

Mr Cuewant shook his head in exasperation, and rolled his eyes at Frank, who had to stifle his laugh with a pretend cough.

"May I politely ask you again. Would you parents please leave the room so that Frank, Peter and Lucy can talk together in private for just a few minutes?" Mr Cuewant asked a bit more patiently.

"I will most certainly not thank you very much! Frank might, might poison my little darling, or, or do something unspeakable to him! - I've read all about you as well Frank Burray in the 'Sun - so it must be true!" Mrs Puginic said, in an angry and not quite so posh voice.

"Er...Sandy, I think we should leave - just let them have a

minute or two together, " said Sirius.

"But-"

"Sandy, *come on.*"

Mrs Puginic let out a huff and a puff and stormed out of the room dramatically. A few moments later, Sirius, Debbie and Gary had left, only the children and Mr Cuewant were now in the room.

"What happened Frank?" Peter immediately asked him. "Because after Sam made me and Lucy fly back into that tree and bang our heads it's all a bit hazy, I, we, sort of only really remember waking up here in bed wearing these turbans! Turned out Mr Cuewant brought us here to be on the safe side in case we had concussion or something!"

"Well..." Frank said, and taking a deep breath he began...

After Frank had told them everything that had happened, Peter and Lucy laid back against their pillows in utter disbelief, but slowly digested everything Frank had just said.

"I told you Sam was a vampire!" Peter said quietly.

"I thought something was strange about that boy as well," Mr Cuewant said. They were all quiet for a minute or so then thinking their own thoughts, when Frank suddenly asked:

"What time is it?!"

Mr Cuewant glanced at his watch and said, "Half past seven.

Better get you back home, Lucy and Peter, this may be the last time I see you until your third year so, well, goodbye..."

Frank said, "Er...OK, well, bye then, you two, hope you have a quick recovery," and grabbed hold of Mr Cuewant's arm.

They disappeared from the hospital wardroom and reappeared in the familiar surroundings of the shed Frank lived in.

"Well, I'd better go then, see you tomorrow, Frank," Mr Cuewant said and disappeared in a breeze of wind.

Frank dropped onto his bed. He was exhausted. He closed his eyes and thought, *only seven lives left.* It didn't take long for him to fall asleep and when he did, he dreamed about all the things he had done so far that year...

Chapter 17- Frangini's Warning

As well as his dreams, Frank had a nightmare that night, but a different kind. It started as one dream with several flashbacks and this is what he saw...Slake stabbing the knife into Mr Cuewant's leg...Tambos the dragon breathing fire at him...the Elf Chamber going into total darkness...the voices in the slide...Slake falling off the the edge of the cliff...Peter and Lucy in the hospital...Slake getting sacked...the snake at the Spelling Bee...Frank then woke up, his Man U duvet was on the floor and his pyjamas were soggy in places with sweat.

It was half past seven by the time Frank had got up out of bed, got dressed and eaten his breakfast. *What can I do for fifteen minutes? Er...read my book!* So he did, he took his thick *Harry Potter* book out and started to read, he only had about one-hundred pages left when he set off for school, leaving the book on his bed. The Tuesday morning sky was filled with dark clouds, the wind was howling and it was especially cold.

"Come on, Frank, sit down," Mr Anderson said when he got into the classroom.

Frank sat down in the unoccupied seat at the back of the room and waited. It was quite boring as neither Peter or Lucy came to school on the Tuesday, Wednesday and Thursday. Maths had become even more boring; Mr Yurt was just talking about geometry and angles while art was even worse. The school's new (well until next year) art teacher was called Mrs Sponge and all she talked about were patterns, it would have been a bit better if Peter and Lucy were there. Mr Cuewant hadn't really showed himself around the school since the hospital visit, but apparently some second-years had seen him earlier rushing down one of the corridors. Rumours abounded around the school that there would be a massive assembly in which everyone from first to sixth-years would have to participate in. *"Apparently Mr Cuewant's holding a massive party!"* Frank heard Richard say, one of his fellow Lions.

And soon came Friday afternoon. Excitement was rising in the school and everyone got into the line in Mr Anderson's classroom quickly.

"No talking on the way there," Mr Anderson repeated his daily mantra.

When the children were let out of the class, they speed-walked down the corridor and arrived at the Enchanted Hall panting.

"Sit down everyone," Mr Cuewant said cheerfully.

To the childrens' surprise, instead of lots of mini tables, there were three, long tables, with benches ready to be sat on. After everyone was seated, Mr Cuewant stood up.

"Hello children! As you already know, you'll be leaving at two o'clock today so we've only got, blimey! Only forty-five minutes for today's assembly, well, should I say, today's...*celebration!*" Mr Cuewant said happily.

"As you may know, there have been various football matches played. Our first-years may have a chance to play next year but...we have counted the points from the younger league, and our older league. This will be a celebration for the champions, you'll also get a trophy in your head-of-house's office," (Lions head-of-house was Miss Spain). "I will now announce the winners."

People shifted uncomfortably in their seats while others just crossed their fingers.

"In third place, are the...SCORPIONS!" The Scorpions looked at their feet disappointingly while Snakes stared menacingly at the Lions. "And now, the moment you've all been waiting for, the house champions are by only one point...LIONS!"

A roar of triumph erupted in the hall while the Snakes and Scorpions looked glum and depressed. Triumphant brass band music started playing 'We Are The Champions' and all the Lions sang it loudly, most of them out of tune, as the main lights dimmed and were replaced by colourful flashing disco lights. When the riotous singing was dying down Mr Cuewant bellowed over it:

"FRANK BURRAY, MY OFFICE AS SOON AS POSSIBLE, PLEASE."

It couldn't be that bad, he'd never been shouted at by Mr

Cuewant and he hadn't done anything wrong as far as he knew.

He got up not looking at anyone and hurried out of the hall. He knocked on Mr Cuewant's door and heard an allowance to enter. He pushed open the dark green door to find Mr Cuewant sitting down already.

"There you are! Come on, sit down, I'm sure you want to get back to the celebration," Mr Cuewant said.

Frank closed the door and sat opposite to Mr Cuewant who was surveying him carefully.

"Now, where to start? I'm very sorry for dragging you out of the party but I'm desperate to tell you something in private, and have no interruptions - as everybody else is now in the hall. I have four things to tell you, so I'll start of with the news of Peter and Lucy," Mr Cuewant said calmly. "Sadly, Peter is suffering with a broken arm and Lucy, a broken ankle, their head wounds are healed though. They're OK, but won't be able to go and run about and do whatever you kids do nowadays, their recovery will take a few weeks, but they'll be back for your second year.

Next thing, Frangini and the Elves have sent an invitation to me addressed to you, they are having a celebration because of you-know-what," Mr Cuewant's went into a whisper, "...The Stone. And they'd love you to attend so...do you want me to let them know you will be?"

"Yeh, OK, great, thanks!"

"They were wanting Peter and Lucy to be there as well, but...well, they can't, so I'll take you there shortly after two o'clock." Mr Cuewant said.

"Now what else...? Er...oh yes! Since you destroyed the stone, have you been having weird dreams...even nightmares?"

Frank had been waiting for this moment, "Er...yeh, I have! And last night's was a bad one! What do they mean?"

"It means you are, well...you're kind of...cursed, to put it bluntly, you've destroyed the first Vouscer, and your help will be needed to destroy the others. I, of course will help you, but...don't go looking for the Vouscers on your own, alright? Only when I come back in your third year, have some time off from it!" Mr Cuewant said seriously.

"Last thing, Frank. The school governors have finally decided who is going to be the new Headmaster.. It's all over the front page of the Severor Sun... here," he chucked the paper at Frank's chest and he read it. "That's him," Mr Cuewant was pointing at a large colour photo of a man in the middle of the page, he had a big bald head and a stubbly beard.

The headline above it read: *'Our New Headmaster! - Paul Spiky-Smooth!* Frank giggled at his surname, *'Spiky-Smooth'* while Mr Cuewant just smiled.

"A lot of changes will be taking place next year when Paul takes over. I'll tell you one, he can't stand 'Mr' or 'Miss' or 'Mrs' so...for instance, he'll insist on being called, *'Professor Spiky-*

Smooth', and he'll insist that pupils call all the other members of staff 'Professor' as well."

Frank couldn't believe what he was hearing, he'd never had to call anyone 'Professor' so this would be a shock when the school finds out.

"Er...right...if that's what he wants! Mr Cuewant, can I ask you something?"

"Certainly - go ahead."

"Well, when we were going to the hospital, how did you walk so fast when you'd been stabbed in the leg just before?" Frank asked him curiously.

"My powers helped me - and that 'growing water' from Shadrik's watering can helped a lot as well, useful stuff, it's a menace though if it spills onto weeds, they turn into a jungle in an hour or so…!" Mr Cuewant chuckled.

"So, I'll see you back in here at two o'clock, and then it's off to the Elves!"

Frank got up and strolled back into the darkened Hall with flashing coloured lights and disco music beating out loudly. Jack, Sadio, Seb and their other fellow Snakes were sat sulking in a dark corner, the Scorpions doing the same in another, but the Lions, well – they were all up on their feet dancing energetically!

After around twenty-five minutes of non-stop dancing to the

loud music, Mr Cuewant brought it all to a stop, and stood up to address the now silent Hall.

"Now...Finally, before you all go, I need to mention a few things that have happened this week, concerning Mr Slake, Mrs Rose and Sam Matthews." Mr Cuewant became very still and then calmly said: "Mr Slake, unfortunately, died this week, and so did Sam Matthews."

Gasps of shock burst out all over the Hall.

"I wondered where Sam was!" Harry said, surprised.

"Mrs Rose, however, I'm relieved to say, is still with us, but unfortunately she has, er, some mental problems, so she's being treated for them in St Plange's. It's quite possible she'll make a full recovery in time, and we all hope she will of course. I'd also like to mention Peter Puginic and Lucy Dart, Peter has broken his arm and Lucy has a broken ankle," the Snakes all livened up on hearing that, especially Jack, Sadio and Seb.

"We all wish them a quick recovery…

"Rightio everyone! I hope you'll all have a wonderful year next year, I know for some of you this one's been a little scary at times, some of it challenging and some of it adventurous. I won't be here next year, but that gives no excuse not to obey all of your new Headmaster's rules and regulations. I'll be back the year after.

"So, that's it from me! - Have a lovely holiday everyone, and don't let me down next year!" he looked down at his watch, "it is now, officially the Summer Holidays! So...You May... Leave...! Goodbye everyone!"

A massive cheer erupted in the Hall. Frank headed for Mr Cuewant's office and to his great surprise, he was already waiting for him when he got in there.

"Hold on to my arm Frank," he said, and they disappeared together from the school and reappeared in the center of the Elf Chamber!

"MR FRANK!" A very loud voice blasted out of a massive speaker that had been put at the top end of the cave and Teethy was shouting excitedly through it. "IT'S MR FRANK! HE'S COME! MASTER, MASTER, EVERYONE - LOOK! MR FRANK HAS COME!"

Frangini's weak voice came out of the crowd of Elves, most of them had their fingers stuck in their ears - due to the volume of Teethy's delighted shouting.

"Thank you, Teethy - I'll soon be deaf if you keep shouting through that speaker! Wish I'd never allowed it!" he said rubbing his ears..

"PARDON ME MASTER WHAT DID YOU SAY I CAN'T HEAR YOU?!" Teethy's amplified voice boomed out again. Frangini shook his head and ignored him...!

"Hello, Frank, we are so grateful to you and because of your fantastic actions, we're throwing a party and you are our guest of honour! The Elf Chamber is no longer cursed thanks to you!"

A cheer and wave of applause erupted in the Elf Chamber. Teethy's clapping sounded like thunder and a volcano erupting at the same time as it was amplified at full volume through the huge speaker, causing the other Elves' clapping to stop as they quickly put their fingers back in their ears. Frangini leaned over to an Elf next to him, pulled his finger out of his ear and told him to go and pull the plug out of the speaker before Teethy made them all go deaf!

"Bring out the food and drink!" Frangini shouted, but the Elves couldn't hear him as they still had their fingers in their ears so he mimed eating and drinking – which they understood and the kitchen Elves dashed off. Frangini quickly made the long, foam table, using only hand gestures and a sort of humming.

"Frank, come and sit next to me - so glad you made it!" Frangini beamed at him.

Before Frank could say something polite in reply, the table was made and he was staring at a large punch bowl filled with a golden drink with froth bubbling on it and dripping down the glass sides.

"What is that?" Frank asked Frangini pointing at the mysterious drink.

"Butterbeer," Frangini said. "Wizards drink it a lot."

"Wizards are real?" Frank asked him, and said he'd only read about them in his fantasy *Harry Potter* book.

"Oh yes, it's quite true, there are hundreds of wizards in England, they're all over the place, people you'd never suspect - you just don't know..." Frangini said. "Wanna try some?"

Frangini passed Frank a glass mug of Butterbeer.

"It tastes a little bit like less-sickly-butterscotch," Frangini said.

It did. Frank sipped some and it tasted exactly like the description Frangini had told him, and it was warm.

"Mmm...Nice!"

There were also lots of different party and sugary foods now on the table: sandwiches, crisps, toffees, sticky buns, nearly everything Frank thought of as party food was on the table.

"START THE FEAST! Help yourself, Frank..."

"Wait, where's Mr Cuewant?" Frank asked realising he had not seen Mr Cuewant since he had left his office with him.

"Left before you opened your eyes, he's very busy today, we'll save him some butterbeer!" Frangini said stuffing a ham and cheese sandwich into his mouth.

With that question answered, Frank put as much food on his

plate as possible – as usual he was hungry! Teethy then came running up to him, holding a present.

"Teethy has bought you this!" he squeaked.

Frank opened the badly-wrapped present and found a pair of red woolly socks and a matching red woolly hat.

"Teethy is pleased with Mr Frank for destroying the Enchanted Stone, put them on!"

Frank stuck the hat onto his head and his socks on his feet. Teethy looked up at Frank with watery eyes and started sobbing uncontrollably.

"Teethy, what's wrong?" Frank asked, perplexed.

"Teethy...wants – Mr - Frank – to - wear - his – socks - on – his - ears!" Teethy wailed.

The other Elves were looking over at Frank and Teethy.

"OK, OK!"

Frank slipped the woolly red socks off and stuck them onto his ears. Teethy quietened down and looked up at Frank, smiling. Then he ran up the spiral staircase and back upstairs. Elves had been queuing up to shake Frank's hand when he wasn't stuffing himself, and by seven o'clock, he'd tried nearly everything on the table and shook the hand of nearly every Elf in the chamber.

Frank needed some fresh air, he'd not left the cave at all since he arrived there hours ago. But there was one problem: he didn't know how to get outside.

"Frangini? Parry, where's Frangini?" Frank asked Parry, the nearest Elf to him.

"Master is in his room," Parry replied.

"Thanks."

Frank couldn't do more than walk slowly up the steps to Frangini's room because he was full of the party food. He got there eventually and swung the door open to room eight hundred. Frangini was sitting in his chair, clutching a bottle of Butterbeer in his hand.

"Hello, Frank! What is it?" Frangini said lively.

"Er...well, I was wondering if I could get some fresh air?"

"As you mention it, I do need some air as well, come on, grab my arm," Frangini yawned.

He led Frank through a small door in his room, walked a few paces, and then stopped. They were now in a very narrow room with a deep trench a few feet wide in front of them, a ladder was on the other side of it

"Step across, but for heaven's sake, do not fall in, I don't know where it goes to," Frangini said.

I don't know where it goes to, what does that mean? Frangini jumped across and clutched onto the ladder, looked back at

Frank saying, "jump across and come up when I shout you."

Frank watched him disappear up the ladder, waited a few seconds and then he heard him shout,

"Ready! - Come up!."

He ran and leaped across, not looking down. Once he was safely on the other side clutching the ladder with both hands, only then did he look down into the trench pit of darkness. Then he started to climb up the ladder. Frangini was quite high above him and all of a sudden, the door they had entered through shut with a loud bang. The narrow room went into darkness but soon lightened up when red and green lights came on.

"Just keep on going, Frank," Frangini's voice echoed.

By the time Frank and Frangini had emerged from the top, they were both panting. Cold, fresh air blew into Frank's face, and he realised that he was on a wooden planked balcony, high up in the air, at the top of a large oak tree. Frank looked at the amazing sunset sky of pink and orange, and the dark clouds swirling underneath it. He was quite gobsmacked!

"Wow," he whispered in awe.

"Nice, isn't it? It's my private tree house." Frangini said. "I'm really happy with you and I've brought you here to tell you about these nightmare-"

"Mr Cuewant's already told me," Frank mumbled.

"Has he now?" Frangini said. "My brother, you know, you shouldn't worry about him. He won't lose his place as Headmaster until he decides to retire."

"He already has, next year, Mr Spiky-Smooth, er, *Professor* Spiky-Smooth, will be the new Head."

"He hasn't been sacked though, has he?" Frangini corrected him.

"No he hasn't – you're right!" Frank smiled at him.

"Paul Spiky-Smooth, what an idiot he is! Trust me, Frank. Paul is thick, thickety thick! He was such a toady nerd at school, not surprised he's had his head shaved with that name. *'Spiky-Smooth'*. Just don't go getting on his bad side, he'll delight in punishing you. If you are ever again in a life-threatening 'seconds-away-from-death-type-moment', he wouldn't lift a finger to save you. He's a toady coward, always was, always will be. You'll agree with me when you've spent even a few minutes with him." Frangini shook his head in disgust.

"He worked, well he still works, for the Severor Sun and he believes absolutely everything they print in that false news rag.. He'll put anything he bothers to find out - or usually he just makes it up - into a letter addressed to the editor of the Severor Sun to be published straight away!" Frangini said, disgust in his voice..

"Oh," Frank was quite shocked and dismayed at all this.

"Don't worry about it, I'm sure it'll be fine, just wanted to let you know – forewarned is forearmed and all that! Well, during the Summer holidays I'll keep in touch with you," Frangini said. "Tell Peter and Lucy I hope they get better soon."

"Uhh, I can't really."

"Oh? Why not?"

"Well, they're in the hospital, and I can't walk there, it's miles away," Frank shrugged.

"Ah well...If anything weird happens, or you are suspicious about anything next year, contact me straight away. Maximus will be wanting information like that, especially after this year, what with everything that has happened – and then finding out a goblin had kidnapped a teacher and was teaching art in her place for nearly the whole year! He was pretty annoyed that you didn't tell him your suspicions sooner! But, you're still young, can't blame you! You've still to learn that things aren't often what they seem to be!" Frangini said calmly.

"Can we go back down now?" Frank asked, wanting to get back into the party mood.

"We can, in a few minutes."

"As I was saying, Maximus and I actually used to go to school with Paul Spiky-Smooth," Frangini said.

After about fifteen minutes of listening to some amusing and some hair raising incidents and embarrassing stories about

Spiky-Smooth, the last one being when Frangini had told Frank how he and Maximus had once tied him to a tree in the forest and left him there - the teachers eventually finding him after searching all day - and giving them a months detention, Frank was getting cold and tired.

"OK, I'm going back inside," Frank yawned widely and turned towards the small door.

No answer...Frank looked back blankly at Frangini whose hair was blowing in his eyes.

Frangini was looking into the gathering dark clouds, and said in a whisper, "Frank...oh dear me....something's coming, something powerful, something dangerous, something dark..."

(To be continued…!)